The Lady Killer

Also by Masako Togawa

The Master Key

The Lady Killer

MASAKO TOGAWA

Translated from the Japanese by

SIMON GROVE

†

DODD, MEAD & COMPANY

New York

First published in the United States in 1986

Copyright © 1963 by Masako Togawa
Translation copyright © 1985 by Simon Grove

Published by Dodd, Mead & Company, Inc.
79 Madison Avenue, New York, N.Y. 10016
Manufactured in the United States of America
Translation originally published in Great Britain
by Century Hutchinson, 1985.
First Edition

3   4   5   6   7   8   9   10

Library of Congress Cataloging-in-Publication Data

Togawa, Masako, 1933–
  The lady killer.

  I. Title.
PL862.03R913   1986   895.6'35   86-6289
ISBN 0-396-08795-7

CONTENTS

PROLOGUE · 1

PART 1 : *The Hunter*

    THE FIRST VICTIM (NOVEMBER 5) · 30

    THE SECOND VICTIM (DECEMBER 19) · 57

    THE THIRD VICTIM (JANUARY 15) · 73

    INTERVAL · 94

PART 2 : *Collecting the Evidence*

    THE LAWYERS · 99

    THE BLOOD BANK · 132

    THE BLACK STAIN · 180

    INSERTION—A MONOLOGUE · 198

    THE BLACK STAIN—CONTINUED · 201

EPILOGUE · 215

The action of this novel is set in Japan in 1963.

PROLOGUE

She was on the second floor of the bar, seated alone in a box seat and gazing down onto the first floor. Faintly, through the whirl of cigarette smoke, she could see a waiter in a white jacket standing by the door, a bartender rattling a cocktail shaker behind the counter below her. As for the other customers, they were all either seated at the counter or else in boxes on the first floor, almost invisible in the subdued lighting popular in such places. Upstairs where she was, there was another bar counter behind which a bartender was passing the time polishing glasses; at the corner of the counter, two young men sat face to face whispering to each other.

Nobody was paying her any attention whatever. If they had, they would have probably thought that this girl, wearing no makeup and seeming to be no more than twenty, did not look at all like a typical bar customer.

When she had entered a few minutes before, there had

been an oddly disturbed look on her face. There were no vacant places on the ground floor, so she had made her way upstairs. As she climbed, the stairs beneath her feet seemed to rise and fall like waves; she floated on them, feeling hollow as a boat. All the chatter and music, the din of a busy bar, seemed to recede from her; she felt strangely alone in a world as black as pitch.

She stretched forward and picked up her half-empty glass, draining its contents, the color of cold tea, in a gulp. This was her third glass of whiskey tonight, and the third she had drunk in all her life. The whiskey warmed her throat, and she began to feel light-headed. She stood up and went to the counter, taking care with each step not to reel or fall.

The bartender looked up and, seeing the empty glass in her hand, smiled.

"Some pace tonight!"

She smiled back at him. It would cost her nothing to be pleasant to him, and besides, she had no idea of where she would go when she left the bar.

"Ready for the fourth one? I'll bring it over." He pretended to note the drink on her bill, but in reality wrote nothing. She might as well have this one free.

Giving him another sweet smile, she turned and went back to her table on the balcony. She suddenly felt more cheerful, thanks to this act of kindness, which she had noticed. *I must give him a pack of cigarettes before I go*, she thought.

The bartender came over, deposited her drink and a fresh

saucer of peanuts, and left her as silently as he had come. Once more, she was alone.

When she closed her eyes, she saw clashing shades of red and green still, but fortunately the sharp metallic sound that had rung inside her head had abated. After a while, she heard music, but it was impossible for her to tell if the sounds came from outside or were merely in her head. She didn't really care which was the case; drifting through her personal world, she beat time with the tips of her feet. One two three, one two three . . . she became aware that the music was a cheerful polka, the instruments a violin and a guitar.

How I used to love this tune, she thought. *Back in the days when I had no worries; I was happy then.* She began to cry silently, moved by this sentimental thought. As she wept, the tune changed; first there was a waltz, and then music of an indeterminate rhythm.

And then she heard the bass voice that she would never forget until the day she died. There was something more than human about it; it was more like an organ heard in church. It crept toward her, lapped her feet and climbed steadily until it captured her heart. She recognized the song; it was "Zigeunerliedchen" by Schumann.

Im Schatten des Waldes, im Buchengezweig,
Da regt's sich und raschelt und flüstert zu gleich.
Es flackern die Flammen, es gaukelt der Schein
Um bunte Gestalten, um Laub und Gestein.

Having completed the first stanza in German, the voice went back to the beginning again and sang in Japanese.

> *Here 'neath the beeches' greening shade*
> *We feast and frolic in the glade.*
> *The torches burn and brightly light*
> *Us sitting on the leaves tonight.*
> *Sing, sing, the greenwoods ring,*
> *The gypsy tribe is frolicking!*

The deep, sad voice was full of soulfulness and sympathy, overriding the thick tones of drunkards and the off-key soprano voices of the hostesses who were endeavoring to accompany it. Who could it be? She opened her eyes, which she had closed in ecstasy, and peered over the railing that surrounded the balcony. But all she could see were two strolling musicians, one with a violin, the other with a guitar, who had accompanied the song. Shyly she too began to sing the "Zigeunerliedchen," which had been a compulsory piece at her high school. Her voice seemed to blend perfectly with the bass. They sang together, they were silent together, in a perfect harmony that she could not leave, until at last the guitar and the violin were silent, the bass, too, fading away.

Who could this singer have been, she wondered, whose voice so matched hers? Unable to restrain her curiosity, she got up and went downstairs, drawn by the magic voice, no freer than a puppet on a string. As she descended to the first floor, her body was drenched by the hubbub; she peered uncertainly into the unaccustomed dark, but all she could make out through the spirals of smoke were the black heads of the crowd, each one seeming to overlap its neighbor. What was she to do?

And then she had an inspiration. The itinerant violinist was about to leave the bar; she rushed over and blocked his way.

"Excuse me, sir! Would you mind playing that again?"

"Of course, young lady, as often as you wish." The violinist, whose hair receded to the crown of his head, gazed curiously into her eyes, his glance also taking in the hundred-yen note that she was proffering. Accepting the tip, he called his partner back; they began to play, and out of the dark and over the babble of voices once again emerged that superb bass voice. The owner turned out to be a man buried in the shadows, sitting alone in the box just behind her. She craned around, trying to see him without seeming too curious.

"Why don't you sit with me?" said the deep voice, and she obeyed as if it was the most natural thing in the world. It felt almost as if they were meeting by prior agreement.

"Keep playing!" he called out, and the man and the girl sang together in perfect harmony.

As they sang, they stole glances at each other; it was as if they had been friends for years.

"Come on, let's have something else for a change!" cried another customer.

The violin player lowered his instrument and asked, "What shall I do? O.K. to play something else?"

She looked at her companion, and then turned back to the musician.

"No, that's enough, thanks. You can go."

And shortly afterward she left, too, in the company of the stranger, who settled her bill as well as his own. As they walked out of the bar together, the light of a streetlamp fell on him, and for the first time she could see him clearly. He was about thirty, she judged, and had a well-tanned, clean-cut face. His suit was both tasteful and well cut. Although he had the appearance of a maiden's dream, she felt regretfully, they must seem to others to be an ill-matched couple.

Several hours later, they sank together into the back seat of a taxi. By now, he was clasping her thin body in his long arms, nuzzling her hair with his chin.

"Take us somewhere where we can get a good night's sleep," he said to the driver. His voice sounded exhausted, almost monotonous.

"Yes, sir. Western or Japanese style?" The driver plunged dangerously into the traffic. Perhaps she heard the exchange between her partner and the taxi driver, perhaps she did not. She lay motionless in his arms, her eyes tightly closed.

2

She was hanging on to the windowsill with her hands but her mind was elsewhere, remembering her encounter at the bar six months ago. A cold breeze chilled her bare feet.

I don't regret having slept with him, she thought. For in her daily life, which had come to seem like hell to her, that one encounter stood alone, a perfect experience.

She hung against the rough concrete wall; it pressed hard on her nose, her cheeks, her small breasts, and her swelling belly, all the way down to her knees. As each moment passed, her body seemed to pull more heavily on her skinny arms. Once her arms could no longer take her weight, once her already numb fingers gave way to the strain, she would let go and fall from this seventh-floor window. Only a little more patience was needed—perhaps two minutes, perhaps three. . . .

She wondered why the man with the deep voice had withdrawn from her life after that one encounter. And yet she felt no grudge against him for it; rather, she was grateful, for into her short, gray life he had brought the only light ever to shine on it.

He was not responsible for the growing pain in my ring finger, she thought. *And every evening, when dusk falls, it seems as if the right half of my body belongs to someone else. But he is not to blame for that, either.* It was tapping those keys, thousands of times a day, which was responsible, not the man. *I owe it to him that I was able to bear to live for another six months*, she thought. *Memories of his voice gave me the will to carry on. I could survive the ringing in my head, like an amplified motorcycle, because of that voice that seemed to put cotton wool into my inner ears, blocking out the sound. The bass voice overwhelmed me, body and soul. But why did he plant his seed in me and then go away?* To this last question she had no ready answer.

She felt the child stir in her belly. Was it this power inside her that was so oppressive, she wondered, or was it the pressure of the wall?

Her arms were now completely numb. If only she could see him in her mind's eye again, hear his voice, then perhaps she could endure the torture for a little longer. But try as she would, he was gone, and his image was lost to her. Instead, inside her head she heard those other sounds begin again, faintly at first, like the droning of a swarm of midges. And her vision was restricted to the coarse concrete wall.

Suddenly, for the first time she felt terror: the surge of fear of her impending extinction. Frantically, she tried to grip the windowsill more tightly, but it was no good; her fingers had lost all sensation. Her arms were numb, too, her shoulders dead. The chill wind blew up under her dress, freezing her lower parts into insensitivity. One by one, her fingers let go of the sill.

Now that romantic encounter at the bar with the man with the rich bass voice was forgotten. Forgotten, too, the nagging presence in her belly. In those last moments, she was wafted back to her primary school days, when she had hung from the beam, trying to chin herself yet again, every muscle in her body aching. How long every second had seemed then, how long now . . .

Last of all, the calloused finger that should one day have worn a wedding ring slipped and lost its grip. All contact with reality lost, she plunged to the earth below.

*   *   *

The shattered body of Keiko Obana, aged nineteen, a key-punch operator working for the K Life Insurance Company, was found by the side of the building by a security guard working for that company just after 1 P.M. on Adults' Day, January 15, a public holiday.

Was it suicide? Or was it, perhaps, murder? There was much discussion until the police announced their conclusion. After the autopsy they declared that it was suicide caused by neurosis. They found that her ring finger exhibited a mild case of tendonitis, the occupational disease of key-punch operators.

The evidence of the security guard was that, although it was a holiday, he had let Keiko Obana into her office as she had said that she wanted to copy some sheet music for her choral group. The official view of the company was naturally to deny the possibility of suicide, for there was no sign of a suicide note. The room had been sprayed with a strong insecticide shortly before; Keiko must have tried to open the window, they reasoned, and had fallen to her death.

However, the police had two reasons for determining that this was a case of suicide. Firstly, there were the marks on the windowsill, which clearly showed that she had hung from it before falling.

And secondly, there was evidence that was not made public. At the time of her death, she was six months pregnant.

Although that would have convinced everybody that the police were right, not a word was allowed to leak to the press on this point. This decision was made by the section chief in the local police station who was in charge of the Keiko

Obana case. He did so on grounds of delicacy, and the only person to whom he revealed the fact of Keiko's pregnancy was the sole surviving relative, her elder sister, when she came to receive the body.

"Did she have a fiancé or anything like that?" he asked in a roundabout sort of way. The sister sat opposite him, wringing her handkerchief between her hands.

"No, not that I was aware of. She never said anything about getting married. She never even mentioned a boyfriend. Of course, she may have kept silent out of deference to me; I am still single, you see. But . . . you know, she was still very much like a child."

The sister looked up at the police officer dubiously.

"You were like a mother to her, were you not?"

"Yes. Both our parents were killed by the atom bomb at Hiroshima. I brought her up and supported her from my income as a dressmaker. She fully understood how hard it was for me, and always did her best not to cause me any worry. And I think she always told me everything."

The elder sister, Tsuneko Obana, was a spinsterish type, simply dressed, with no makeup, and her hair drawn back in a bun. There was something faintly erotic about her double-lidded eyes, but otherwise she seemed to have no more than a stoic personality. She sat with her head inclined downward and seemed overcome with grief at her sudden bereavement.

To lose one's only sister in this way was indeed tragic, thought the inspector, and he tried to temper his questions as far as possible.

"Did you notice anything special about her?"

"What do you mean? Is there something I should know?" She looked at him uncertainly.

"Well, for instance, did she occasionally stay out all night?"

"Oh, no, never . . . but yes, once only. She came home in the morning and said that she had missed the last train and had spent the night at an all-night café with a friend."

"About when would that have been?"

"Well, let me see . . . about six months ago, I think it was. But does that have any bearing . . . ?"

"Well, yes, I'm afraid it does. I'm sorry to have to tell you this but your sister was pregnant."

The sister's eyes almost popped out of her head with shock. "I can't believe it," was all she could say.

"Yes. She was, in fact, six months pregnant. I think the worry made her kill herself."

Tsuneko Obana burst into tears. The inspector averted his eyes; it had been hard for him, but he felt he had to tell her. He gazed out of the window. If Keiko had been a respectable young woman, as seemed to have been the case, if she was a girl with no boyfriends who came home every night, then on that night she spent in the all-night café she must have been seduced by a gangster or some such person. There were only too many such cases of which he was aware. Normally, they were about as emotional as traffic accidents, but in this case the girl had killed herself. What could he say to soothe the sister now that the truth was out? Nothing. He turned his gaze back upon the sister.

"Naturally, the police are only informing you of this fact. I can assure you that it will never be made public."

After all, he reasoned, if the suicide could be attributed to a vocational disease, then the relatives could claim compensation.

Tsuneko Obana dabbed her face with her handkerchief, trying to repress her tears. Suddenly, she looked up and began to speak urgently, as if a dam had broken inside her.

"She did have a lover. . . . I read her diary. . . . She met him in a bar . . . and they sang 'Zigeunerliedchen' together. . . . How could she be so stupid? . . . Poor, foolish girl . . . "

There was nothing he could say, the inspector thought, as he listened to these disjointed statements. He stood up to bring the interview to an end. The sorrow of bereaved relatives does not lie within the jurisdiction of the police.

"Well, that is all, Miss Obana. I have no more questions to ask you."

As she collected her belongings and made ready to go, he noticed for the first time that she had a very distinctive mole on the edge of one nostril. It had been hidden by the handkerchief, but now he could see it clearly. She caught his eye, and, embarrassed by his rudeness, he quickly looked away.

"I am sorry for the trouble you have been caused." The sister mouthed the appropriate formula, but left the police station looking overwhelmed with grief.

As he watched her leave, the inspector was seething with anger. He felt his chest tighten with rage against the unknown man who had so casually made a nineteen-year-old girl pregnant. The fact that the man was unknown made his pent-up wrath the greater. *If it was my daughter,* he thought, *I would hunt the man down, root him out, and give him just punishment for such a crime.*

Of course, in such a case, it would be at least as hard to find the man as to identify a murderer. The thought depressed him. There was really nothing that could be done; he began to regret that he had told the sister, so pointlessly, of Keiko's pregnancy.

THE HUNTER

I

In summer, the bars and small restaurants in Kabuki-cho, Shinjuku, usually greet the first customers of the day at about 4 P.M. However, trade at this hour is listless; the place has only just opened, and the air conditioner has not begun to bite, or else the floors are still glistening with fresh-sprinkled water. The customers huddle at the end of the counter and get on with the serious business of drinking; they certainly do not revel at that hour or spend money on itinerant street musicians.

These wandering minstrels usually turn up in the entertainment districts after 8 P.M. But on a certain day a violin player known since his youth as "Ossan"—"the old fellow"—set out early and was cruising the area by 6 P.M., when the sun was still high in the sky. This was because he had taken the previous day off and needed the money. Both the old fellow's low-heeled shoes, the soles of which were worn to paper-thinness, and the sandals of his partner were spattered with white dust.

"Hey! Old fellow!" They were passing the Bar Boi just behind the Koma Theater when a waiter came out and called them. "One of our customers wants music. She says only a violinist will do."

"She really wants a violinist? That's unusual." Nowadays, no one seemed to want violin music, what with the craze for the guitar. They followed the waiter into the cool and almost deserted bar.

He led him to a table where there sat a female customer wearing dark glasses and a wide-brimmed hat. The old fellow bowed to her.

"What would you like me to play, madam?" He studied his client's face carefully, noting the large mole on the side of her nose.

"Can you play 'Zigeunerliedchen'?"

"Ah, now, if you ask me for a classical piece I can play anything you want."

"Go ahead, then, let's hear you." Her voice seemed strangely toneless.

Getting his instrument out of its case, the old fellow reflected that he'd heard of a woman who made this request to some of his colleagues. None of them could play it, which was a pity for them, as the woman offered to pay a thousand yen just to hear that one tune. It must be the same woman, he thought. But the old fellow was a far better hand at the classics than at modern music. The guitarist began to strum, and he embarked upon the haunting melody.

The woman just sat and listened, without making any effort to sing the words. Yet she didn't seem to be drunk, just odd. When they came to the end of the tune, she merely said, "Once more."

He complied, and when he finished he asked, "How about something else?"

But the woman was silent. There was certainly something odd about her: mad, perhaps. Here she was at a Shinjuku bar wearing a large hat and sunglasses, just as if she was on the beach. It was impossible to read the expression on her face, tricked out as she was in that manner.

At last she broke her silence, and when she spoke her voice seemed artificial.

"Do you play that often?"

"Well, it's not a common request."

"But surely you play it sometimes?" The woman spoke almost aggressively, as if trying to force his answer. *I know the type,* the old fellow thought. *Kindergarten teachers, they're like that.*

"I used to play it a lot in the old days."

"But how about recently? How about a year ago, for instance?"

This question was so preposterous that the old man could not prevent himself from laughing.

"Well, if you say so. I mean, I play every day, so I can hardly remember what I played when."

"Surely you remember. It was in this very bar, right?"

"Here?"

"Yes, in the Bar Boi, on the ground floor. A man and a woman sang the song, and only that song, several times over."

"Can you remember?" He turned to his partner, a much younger man with heavily oiled hair.

"Search me." The guitarist plainly did not like her interrogative approach.

She stood up suddenly and pointed to a corner of the room. She had the posture and tone of a prosecutor in court.

"It was over there. There was a man sitting alone who asked for that song. Now think back. He looked a bit foreign—he had very sharp features. You must remember him, he was so handsome."

The two strolling players were astonished. They looked at her in a puzzled manner, but she went on, ignoring their bewilderment.

"He was singing down here. And upstairs there was a young girl. She joined in the singing, and after the first duet she came down and joined him and they sang it again. Surely you can remember! Think! Think!"

The old fellow did his best to remember, but his partner was plainly bored.

"An unforgettable voice," she went on. "Unusually deep—not at all typically Japanese. Now do try and remember. I'm asking about a man with a deep bass voice."

"Ah," said the old fellow in a relieved tone. "You're talking about Mr. Honda. Yes, that's who it will be. Haven't seen him around much recently."

"What does he do for a living, this Mr. Honda?"

"Oh, I really couldn't say. I mean, I address all my customers either as 'professor' or as 'president,' and think no more of it. I used to call him 'professor,' that's all I can tell you. He likes singing, though, and has a good voice. I think he once told me that he was the leader of the choral society when he was at college."

"Which university was that?"

"Now, let me see. A.B.C.—was that it? No, not quite, but it was something like that—three letters of the alphabet. Maybe it wasn't in Japan at all, but overseas, with a name like that."

"Have you seen him around recently?"

"No, come to think of it, not for quite a while. He used to be a regular in the local bars, but not anymore. Moved on to some other area, I suppose."

At this, the woman looked disappointed, but she opened her handbag nonetheless and pulled out a thousand-yen note. As she handed it to them, she added, "If there are any other bars around here where he used to go, please tell me."

"Other bars? Yes, there were one or two; now, let me see." And after a little thought, he reeled off the names of several bars. The woman wrote them down carefully in a notebook and left.

"I suppose it was all right to tell her that much," said the old fellow.

"You mean, maybe she's got it in for the professor and wants to make trouble?"

"Yes, but no need to worry, I suppose. I mean, it was all true, what I said, and nothing bad about him. She didn't look like a policewoman." He pocketed the thousand-yen note. "All that matters is that we got well paid."

Thereafter, whenever he went into one of the bars, the

names of which he had given to the woman, the old fellow always made sure to ask about her, but never with any result.

"No sign of that woman? The one who asked about the professor, the man with the deep bass voice?" Always, the answer was no.

"An odd one, she was. Anyway, we did our best to help. But what's she up to, I wonder?" He racked his brains to no avail. "Well, that's life, I suppose. People are here today, gone tomorrow. Just like the wind, people are. I mean, they go and drink at the same place for a while, and then just vanish. Plenty of cases like that, come to think of it."

"Well," said his young companion philosophically, "that's the entertainment business for you. A chancy trade, with customers always coming and going."

And there they left it. After a while, they forgot all about the inquisitive woman with the mole on her nose.

2

Asia Moral University is located on a hill outside Tokyo, some fifteen minutes by bus from K Station on the Chuo Line. It is generally known as A.M.U.

It stands in broad grounds amidst the woodlands of the plain of Musashi. In the center of the campus stands a fine, three-story building, the center for studies, and in the surrounding grounds there are spacious dormitories for students and the faculty, who all live in. The student body includes many from elsewhere in Asia and even from Africa, so not much Japanese is heard on the campus. English is the most common language used at A.M.U.

The students are allowed out to the local centers of amusement on Sundays and national holidays; otherwise, they pass their lives in this monastic atmosphere concentrating on their studies.

It was at 1 P.M. on the tenth of October that a bus drew up at the bus stop in front of the university, depositing a single female passenger there. The university operates a two-semester system, and it was still vacation time. As the cloud of dust thrown up by the bus settled, the woman removed the handkerchief that she had kept pressed to her face, replacing it in her handbag and straightening the collar of her kimono before moving on.

She walked down the narrow country road for about five minutes, which brought her to the gates and the broad drive leading to the university. She stood there for a while, gazing in, and then, seeming to change her mind, turned and went back the way she had come. Just beyond the bus stop was a shabby store selling candy, bread, cigarettes, and other small necessities of daily life. It also had a public telephone. It was an unprepossessing sort of a shop; a thin film of dust covered the goods. It did not seem likely to attract many customers.

The woman went to the phone and picked up the receiver. Immediately an old crone emerged from the shadows at the rear of the shop, her eyeglasses slipping down her nose.

"Calling Tokyo?" she asked sharply. "If you want long distance, I've got to do it for you."

The woman shook her head and covered her face with her handkerchief. The old woman withdrew into the shadows but continued to watch her. It seemed that the woman was calling the university.

She got through to the switchboard. She had a list of faculty members open in front of her.

"Professor Matsuyama, please. He is responsible for the choral society, isn't he?"

"Yes, madam. Putting you through now."

Saburo Matsuyama, Professor of the History of Church Music, was studying ancient scores in the library when the phone call reached him. Although he was a recognized authority in his field, he was now over seventy, and lecturing was no longer easy for him. He was also rather deaf, and nowadays his chief pleasures were playing the organ and conducting the choral society.

"Hello," he said into the mouthpiece. "Matsuyama here. Who's that?"

"Professor Saburo Matsuyama?"

"Yes, yes, who's that?"

"I am from a matrimonial agency, Professor. I am ringing to inquire about one of your former pupils, a Mr. Ichiro Honda, who I understand used to lead the choral society."

"Speak up, I can't hear you." Although the voice was polite, the woman seemed to be speaking through her nose. She repeated herself twice, raising her voice at the last occasion until he could hear.

"Oh, I see. Yes, ask me whatever you want to know."

Guided by the woman's questions, he began to expatiate

on the university career of Ichiro Honda. Fortunately, Honda had been an excellent student, and the professor remembered him well. Also words of praise, so important on these occasions, came easily to him. He talked enthusiastically of the diligence, the musical aptitude, and even the good looks of his former pupil. What else could he say?

"Oh, yes, there's one other thing I've just remembered, which goes to show what a fine young man he was. Honda has a rare blood type—only about one in several thousand have it, I gather. Yes, well, he donated blood when he was a student and saved the life of a baby. Yes, it was in all the newspapers at the time, I seem to remember. How did we know he had blood in that group? Well, madam, we have an American Institute of Biology here, of which we're very proud, and we note every student's blood type."

"What type was it? Can you tell me?"

"I can't remember exactly. But if you ring the Institute, they'll certainly have it on record."

The professor suddenly realized that having a very rare blood type was not necessarily conducive to marital negotiations and tried to rectify his error.

"Well, an unusual blood type shouldn't affect his married life, you know. Just ring the Institute and they'll tell you. By all means use my name when you talk to them if you like. The switchboard will put you through. By the way, how is Honda nowadays? I gather he went to the United States and studied computer sciences there. I heard that he's working in that field now and is very busy; we haven't seen him for years."

"Ah, yes, well . . . I'll certainly tell him to visit you soon," said the nasal voice hurriedly. She then excused herself and put the receiver down, cutting the professor off.

She dialed again, only this time the old woman could not make head or tail of what she was talking about. It seemed to be about blood, but it was all very complicated. It was not just the complexity of the conversation that was to stick in the old woman's mind, causing her to remember the incident; rather, it was the disagreeable impression left with her by a customer who bought nothing and monopolized the telephone for so long. She watched the woman leave, sliding her glasses up from the tip of her nose, and it was then that the old woman noticed the mole at the base of one nostril.

The old woman was superstitious. Surely, she thought, only great wickedness could be denoted by a mole like that on a woman's face.

It was a few hours later that Professor Matsuyama began to entertain doubts about the phone call.

He was talking to his secretary. "I had an inquiry just now about one of my graduates," he said. "It was from a matrimonial agency."

"Who was it about?"

"Ichiro Honda."

His secretary expressed astonishment. "That's most odd," she said.

"Why?"

"If I remember right, he got married some years back. Let me see. It was when he was in America, wasn't it? A Japanese girl from a rich family, if I remember aright. She was studying at the same university. Quite a beauty, I gather. You're too wrapped up in your work, Professor, that's the trouble with you. Fancy forgetting something like that!"

The professor mumbled something and changed the subject. Come to think of it, he did remember having received a notification of marriage on a beautiful card printed in both Japanese and English some five or six years before.

He went into the corridor outside and gazed across the school grounds. The fine buildings stood serenely in their landscaped surroundings, each casting its shadow in the fading sun. It seemed to him that some dark shadow also lay over his former student, whom he remembered so clearly singing vigorously in the back row of the chorus.

He felt strangely uneasy. Pressing his head against a marble pillar, he began to pray, as a good Christian should, for the safety of his old pupil.

3

"Front desk. Hello!"

Junji Oba, reception clerk at the Toyo Hotel, answered the phone with the soft voice he reserved for business transactions. He moistened his lower lip with his tongue, just in case it was a foreigner and he had to switch to English.

"J.C. Airlines here," said a woman's voice. "Could you give me the room number of a Mr. Honda who is staying with you, please."

"Honda? Yes, certainly. What would his first name be, please?"

"Ichiro. I-chi-ro." She spelled out the three syllables of the name, pausing between each.

Junji Oba was new to the job. He had many years' experience, but an unfortunate error at his last place of work had brought him to the Toyo Hotel. So despite his experience, he was forced to concentrate like a beginner in order to avoid error.

He searched the register diligently, running his fingers down the five-hundred names that were listed floor by floor. Soon he discovered Honda's name—corner room, third floor. Age twenty-nine, Japanese national, occupation engineer.

"Mr. Honda is in room 305," he told the woman. He was about to hang up when the voice came back with an inquiry that was so strange that he had to ask her to repeat herself.

"I said, does he have a low voice?"

"A low voice, did you say? Or did you ask if he is short?"

"Yes, a low voice ... a deep voice ... an unforgettable voice."

The reception clerk thought quickly. What a peculiar line of inquiry. If one wants to confirm that one has the right person, one doesn't normally ask about his voice. One might ask about the person's occupation—Mr. So-and-So of such and such a company, for example. Or Mr. Honda from America, or Mr. Honda from England. And yet this woman said she was from an airline company. So this was not a routine inquiry; it was aimed at research, detective work perhaps. He thought for a moment and remembered an

Oriental with a deep voice amongst the guests, a man who normally spoke in English.

"Yes, I think he does have a low voice. We have so many guests staying, you see . . . it's hard to remember."

"But he really is staying there, isn't he?" The clerk fancied he heard a tone of relief in her voice, as if she had tracked down the man at last after many difficulties. She went on: "Do you know how long he's staying for?"

"Wait a minute and I'll see."

He put down the receiver and checked the reservation for room 305. It turned out that Ichiro Honda was a long-stay guest who had spent the last three months in the hotel. Maybe she'll make it worth my while, Oba thought; he looked around carefully to see that he was not overheard before picking up the receiver again.

"Hello. Mr. Honda is a long-stay guest. I was just thinking, maybe I could give you any information you need face to face. It's not very suitable for the phone, you know. I could meet you somewhere outside and give you good information."

"What do you mean by that?" The woman's tone hardened as if he had put her on her guard.

"Well, I was just thinking . . . I thought that if you wanted, I could possibly . . . I mean, I was just . . . " he stammered, wiping the cold sweat from his forehead.

"All I was asking was how long Honda will be staying for." The voice was relentless. He tried to apologize for his misunderstanding, but to no avail. The woman became sterner and sterner. Now she had even dropped the polite

"Mr." from Honda's name, speaking as if he was a criminal.

"Well, I really don't know what his plans are. All I know is that he has stayed here for three months so far. If you ring again tomorrow, we could ask him what his plans are."

"That will not be necessary," she snapped, but behind her arrogant tone he thought he detected some uncertainty. Plainly, she was from a detective agency or something like that. Maybe she had been put on the job by a business rival, or else a prospective client.

"If you prefer, I could find out without reference to the guest himself. How about that?"

She did not reply, so he went on: "I am Oba, reception clerk. Over the years I've helped a lot of inquiry agents, you know; I usually get a small fee for my services, of course. If you are interested, I go off duty at eight tonight, and I'll be waiting at the coffee shop over the road from this hotel—it's called 'Konto,' and if you ask for me at the desk, they know me. If you're interested, turn up there." And he replaced the receiver rapidly before she could say anything more, but she was too fast for him and hung up even before he did. The negotiation was plainly over, but would she come?

"Lying bitch!" he muttered. Then he looked up and saw a foreign guest approaching the counter. He put on his practiced smile and greeted the customer in English.

Before he went off duty, by dint of inquiry amongst his fellow reception clerks and the room boys responsible for 305 he had acquired some interesting information about Ichiro Honda.

This guest certainly did have a deep voice. Although a

long-stay guest, he paid his own bills in cash. He only used the hotel room to sleep in and usually came back late at night. He was a fluent speaker of English; though his name and appearance were Japanese, he rarely used that language, but was often to be seen conversing with foreigners in the lobby or coffee shop.

Even that should be enough for him to earn some money, Oba thought. And there was one more suspicious circumstance: Mr. Honda always went off somewhere for the weekends. He went to the coffee shop across the road and waited.

At eight forty-five he was called to the phone. He picked up the receiver and heard the same cold voice he had listened to earlier in the day.

"I checked, and your guest Mr. Honda isn't the one I'm looking for, so I won't bother to come and see you."

"But madam!" he spluttered. "There must be some mistake! My Mr. Honda certainly does have a deep voice!"

She said nothing but hung up. He paid his bill, cursing the money wasted on his coffee and cake.

The First Victim (November 5)

The Day Kimiko Tsuda Was Strangled at Minami Apartment at XX, Kinshicho, Koto Ku, Tokyo.

I

He awoke before seven; someone, a traveler with an early start, no doubt, was walking down the corridor wearing slippers. It was now three months since Ichiro Honda moved into the Toyo Hotel.

He reached over to the portable alarm clock on the bedside table and turned off the alarm. Recently, he felt, he had become a light sleeper—just like an old man. Why was this so? He presumed it was because of his nightlife, and particularly his experiences with women.

He got out of bed and, still in his pajamas, went into the bathroom. He followed the same routine every morning. He would take a fresh towel from the rack, dry his face and then crumple the towel like a paper ball and hurl it carelessly into the corner. Self-consciously, like an actor in an American film, he took a suit out of the closet and threw it onto the bed. Little by little he dressed: a well-starched shirt, a slim tie, tasteful and in solid colors; pearl cuff links. He dressed with his usual care. Today, having looked at himself in the

30

mirror, he undid his tie and retied it, but otherwise it was his practiced routine; watching him, one knew that he was an habitué of hotel life.

On the luggage rack there was a blue suitcase covered with first-class stickers from the world's best airlines and the most famous hotels in the United States. It was a very expensive case and his only luggage apart from another case in the closet.

In this hotel, he was known as a long-stay traveler. Even he thought of himself as a traveler. Once a week he would commute to Osaka for a short weekend, and this, too, was traveling. In Osaka he had a wife, Taneko, whom he had married whilst a postgraduate student in the United States. But after they got back to Japan, his wife said that she didn't want to live in Tokyo, this despite the fact that she had been to college there and even had a small part in a professional drama there once. She said that she was happier staying in the parental home in Osaka, so Ichiro Honda spent his weekdays living in a hotel in Tokyo.

Taneko's father was still in good health and continued as President of D Corporation, a top-ranking public company. His wealth had accustomed her to having her own way ever since she had been a child. Now she lived with him and a housekeeper in their large mansion in Ashiya, forcing Ichiro to travel to Osaka and back every weekend. However, she had become accustomed to this style of living, and it seemed to her to be the most natural form of existence. For his part, too, he had come to enjoy a double life where he could enjoy the advantages of a single man for much of the time. Whatever his wife got up to whilst he was away was of no concern to him; he was no more concerned, either, in how she endured her lonely life. Just a month ago, his wife had had a small studio built in a corner of the garden where, the housekeeper told him, she would withdraw for two or three days at a time. If this kept her happy, well, so much the better.

Just as he was not jealous of his wife, so Taneko affected no interest in whatever he did to pass the time in Tokyo. He always flew between the two cities, but he seemed to suffer most from emotional strain whilst he was in Osaka. On his return flights to Tokyo he always looked gloomy, which must in some way have been the fault of his wife. His plane would get into Haneda on Sunday evening. The other passengers would have the light step of people returning home, but not he; he looked more like someone walking in a cortege. He displayed duty and hesitation rather than pleasure. He would take a taxi to the hotel and sit slumped in the back without saying a word; Saturday nights were obviously an ordeal for him. As soon as he got back to the hotel he would go straight to bed—the one night of the week when he did so.

By nine sharp on Monday mornings he would be in his office, a private room on the sixth floor of the K Precision Machinery Company in the center of the business district. He occupied a fairly senior post as a computer specialist in this company. Just as gas companies send out staff to supervise the fitting of boilers and so forth, so he was sent out as a consultant to visit large companies, department stores, insurance companies, canning factories, and the like, advising the clients of the most effective way of solving their problems.

So during the eight hours between nine and five, Ichiro Honda led a blameless life, five days a week, plus the time of his visits to Osaka. As far as the world was concerned, he was a devoted husband and a serious worker. But for him, his real life was bounded by the hours of his freedom in Tokyo in the evenings. Ichiro Honda, the computer specialist married to a rich wife, vanished from the face of the earth in the evenings. At first he had drifted, lonely and bored, and had then taken to finding solace in the arms of women.

Every day, he would go back to his hotel straight after work, to wash, perhaps change, and have dinner: on one day meat, on the next fish, but always a bottle of Bordeaux to wash his meal down. Leaving the dining room, he would saunter into the lobby and read the evening papers, both in English and in Japanese. Some evenings he would enjoy a conversation with an Englishman who occasionally stayed in the same hotel. Honda prided himself on his ability to speak the Queen's English. His favorite topics on these occasions were drama and literature.

At eight o'clock promptly, by which time it was always dark, he would pick up a taxi at the hotel entrance, and his evening would begin. But before getting into the car, he would stand and appreciatively sniff the aroma of Tokyo, which seemed to be compounded of darkness and neon; satisfied that night had indeed once again transformed the city, he would head for the town, for the places where the women awaited him.

His targets were never professional women; rather, they were the lonely and those others who pined for love. To hunt them down, he nightly patrolled music cafés, bars, dance halls, and even cinemas, but all of them away from the business or fashionable entertainment areas. Office girls, sales clerks, typists, beauticians . . . students, even. They all lay in wait for him along the walls of dance halls or seated in coffee shops and cinemas. They lay in wait, but they were his victims; all he had to do was to find them.

To him, women were no more than tinplate targets at a shooting gallery in a fair. The man pulls the trigger, the woman falls, but after all they are made of tinplate and will rise again. So he could go on shooting to his heart's content.

Until such time as the target turned out not to be tin, and blood would be shed . . .

Ichiro Honda had a way with women. He had the faculty of penetrating their psychology at first meeting. Was the woman interested in the arts? Very well, he would be a musician or a painter. In time, he had been sailor, airline pilot, poet, bartender. To hear him in the last role explaining how to mix drinks was enough to make one feel thirsty. And as for his nationality, he had found it effective to represent himself as having come from somewhere outside Japan. His story was that he had been born in England, or Paris, or had spent his boyhood in Chicago. He didn't have to go into much detail—the story itself was usually enough. As a child, his classmates had mocked his foreign looks, but his clean-cut, chiseled features now stood him in good stead.

He even had a British passport, already expired and abandoned by its owner, which he would flash around. It had taken him three days to change the photo and signature and correct the dates, but it was worth it. He was breaking no law; customs or immigration were never involved, just women. He would leave it, ostentatious in its navy blue cover with the gold coat of arms, on a bedside table or on the counter of a bar. Words were quite unnecessary—the woman only had to see it to believe.

Despite his use of such tactics, he was inside himself convinced that women were naturally his prey because of some innate gift, some supernatural sense, that he had been born with. Often he awoke with a premonition of what woman the day would bring him. He could not explain it—it was just there, a blend of the excitement of his mind and the inner rhythms of his body. These foretastes of the evening would occur to him during purely routine activities such as knotting his tie. Not even his work at the office could drive these thoughts from his mind; they lingered with him all day long, so that he felt as if his soul had left his body and was flying around somewhere over his head awaiting the dusk.

On October 15—a day that would be burned into his mind by the subsequent interrogations of the police, the prosecutor, his lawyer, and the judge—such a premonition came over him as he was tying his tie. He retied it carefully; as he picked up his room key, he broke into a cheerful whistle and ran down the stairs two at a time, eschewing the elevator as being too pedestrian for such a day. He read the papers in the lobby, taking his morning tea at the same time, and then went into the dining room and ordered toast and ham and eggs. He glanced at the local news in the press; traffic accidents, double suicides, and murders—what did these have to do with him? All of these human dramas were for him but arrangements of print on the page; he could not foresee his feelings on reading the papers a few weeks later. Did he but know it, he was no more than an insect in flight over whom the net was about to descend. As far as he was concerned, the world took no account of him and his do-ings.

As he walked to the subway, the burden of expectation oppressed his chest. He felt like a hunter setting forth for the field, and the whole world seemed to be bathed in sunlight.

2

On the evening of the fifth of November, Ichiro Honda boarded a bus at Yotsuya Sanchome, arriving at Shinjuku Oiwake. He was clad in a loose-textured tweed coat and hunting cap of the type affected by French film actors in the 1930s. The whole ensemble was brown. He had changed into this outfit at the apartment that he had rented under the assumed name of Shoji Ueda for the last two years. He had gone directly to this apartment, in a building called Meikei-so, immediately after he had left work. The landlord was under the impression that he was a writer who used the apartment to get on with his manuscripts in private.

The flat had two rooms, one about a hundred feet square and the other about seventy-five. Both were in the Japanese style with matted floors, and it served his purpose. For one thing, it was more private than most similar places—the caretaker was not curious, nor were those in the neighboring rooms. Of course, Honda never took anyone else there. The wardrobe was full of suits and coats; there was also a desk and a bed. Here he would always change into whatever costume took his fancy for that night. The decision was not always an easy one between the hunting cap, a trilby, or a French beret; between, say, the sweater with the red lining or a shabby raincoat. Sometimes he would change costumes several times before he was satisfied. Then he would sit down and write his diary.

He called it "The Huntsman's Log," and in it he would record all his adventures with women. He had been keeping it for many years, and the fat notebook was almost full. Such was his routine on days like this when the morning premonition came over him; he would go to the flat, change, and read or write up his diary of conquests.

Reading each entry would recapture for him the remembrance of his successes; he could resavor the taste of each woman. He could evoke the feeling of a breast beneath his hand, or the rustling of an underslip as it slid from a body. Visiting these past experiences would prepare him the better for the pleasures that waited him that night.

On this particular evening, the book fell open at an entry made about a year before. Later, he believed that this was no mere accident, that some hand had guided his, but at the time he thought nothing of it. Reading the passage, he recalled the woman clearly; he saw again her face as she sobered up. She had had a muddy complexion, and her face was cratered with acne scars. His eyes ran down the words he had written in his clear, forceful hand:

July 18
Fierce heat. At 3 P.M. the thermometer read 38 Centigrade. I dirtied my Italian shoes in the melting asphalt in the road between the hotel and work.

I was asked to go for a swim but felt no attraction for the sea and declined.

The heat reminded me of a slack afternoon in a Chicago café some years ago when I just sat and watched the electric fan in the ceiling rotate sluggishly.

I was torn between listlessness and carnal desire. I was particularly attacked by sexual feelings twice at work—once in the morning and once in the afternoon.

Dined at the hotel. The heat, persisting after sunset, conversely cooled my zest for hunting. Went to an air-conditioned cinema but fell asleep after ten minutes. Headed for Shinjuku; drank scotch with water at several bars—Roi, Black Swan, Bon Bon. Found a victim at the fourth place, Boi.

Shot her dead.

38

Report of proceedings.

Strolling musicians came in. Asked them to sing "Zigeunerlied-chen," an old favorite of my schooldays. Surprised when a velvety female alto joined in upstairs. Most dramatic. Sang the song several times. Was stimulated more than I had been for a long time by sensing my victim, invisible upstairs.

Turned out to be a skinny girl. No need to hunt her; she flew straight into my hand. Left Boi and took her to several more places.

Taxi driver took us to an air-conditioned inn where I remember having slept before. Charged me twice as much this time—ridiculous—remember not to go there again.

Prey had a strong head for drink? Anyway, no resistance, no hysterics, no overacting. Just put herself into my hands. Felt like a god accepting a human sacrifice.

Did her best to satisfy my every need, but was too tense and kept trembling. Took two hours to kill. She was a virgin; drew blood.

She slept for three hours, a strangely relieved look on her face. Couldn't think why.

Checked her handbag. Obviously not well off, so slipped in a few thousand yen.

Left inn at 5 A.M. and took prey to Omori by taxi. Had to wake maid at inn—she was in bad mood and accepted my tip with ill grace. My victim noticed and said, "Well, it must be a hard life for her, too."

All her relatives killed by atom bomb; lives with 29-year-old sister at Omori.

> *Keiko Obana*
> *Aged 19*
> *Key-punch operator.*
> *Fujii Apartments, XX Omori Kaigan, Shinagawa-ku.*
> *Employer: K Life Insurance.*

All of above obtained from identity card in her handbag.

POSTSCRIPT
> *Jan. 15.*
> *This victim put an end to her life six months after her affair with me. Newspapers say cause was occupational disease.*
> *Alas, poor Keiko.*

After summoning up the memory of Keiko's face, he turned the page and began to read the next entry. The thought of any connection between himself and the girl who had killed herself after sleeping with him once never crossed his mind. The newspaper articles were but more fuel for an entry in his log.

He remembered watching her receding back going down the narrow alleyway at Omori Kaigan, where the air is full of the fresh smell of the sea. Even he was always hurt by partings; he saw it as the price to be paid for love. He shook his head ruefully. But it was no time for such thoughts—he was ready for the hunt, and dismissed them from his mind.

He went to the cupboard and began to dress with meticulous care. It gave him pleasure to don a dark brown herringbone jacket and to select a deep red bow tie. He chose an overcoat of thick but loose-woven tweed made in Britain. He stood in front of the wardrobe mirror and carefully combed his jet black and slightly wavy hair. After a little reflection, he chose a dark brown hunting cap, and then as an afterthought he deliberately loosened his tie and twisted it slightly off center.

Like most men of his type, he was a narcissist. He examined his face in the mirror, noting with approval his black eyes with their impenetrable depths and their double-folded lids. This was not merely his face; it was a mask for others to see in it what they would. But nonetheless it struck him as a charming face, and he winked at it. The face winked back at him from the mirror.

Outside, the cold winds played at his mufflerless throat, but his feet danced merrily over the pavement. In the lanes not occupied by trams the cars thrust and jostled, so it took some time for him to find a break in the traffic and dart across the road, just in time to catch a crowded bus that arrived at that very moment.

He got off at Shinjuku Oiwake and was immediately attracted by the beauty of a selection of musical instruments arrayed in a brilliantly lit window. It was Kotani, a well-known instrument shop, and he pushed open the door and went in. Within, all was light and gaiety; students, couples, and salaried workers crowded the counters buying audio equipment, records, or musical instruments. His eye quickly picked out a group of office girls gathered around a record stand. Most of them were just over twenty years old, but one woman stood out as being older. Although one of the group, she seemed to detach herself from their gay chatter. They obviously all worked for the same company, and from their conversation he gathered that they were English-language typists. It seemed that someone at their workplace was about to get married, and they were choosing a present.

Watching them, he made up his mind. The old maid would be his target for tonight. He had already sensed in her a mixture of loneliness and irritation. When he heard her decline an offer to go with the younger women to a coffee shop, his mind was made up. He withdrew a little and made himself as unobtrusive as possible whilst watching the group.

Shortly afterward, the woman left the group and made her way to the door. She left the shop alone, and Ichiro followed her.

His victim was smartly dressed in a well-tailored mohair coat of simple design. She looked over thirty, and something in the jut of her chin revealed to him the pride of a woman who lives alone as well as the shadow that overhangs a woman who has lost the chance of marriage. He was ready to begin the night's hunt.

He followed her, knowing from her conversation that she was headed for Shinjuku Station. There should be plenty of time to overtake her and engage her in conversation. So far, his premonitions had never let him down; everything always went smoothly. So it would be tonight.

He caught up with her at the pedestrian crossing just in front of Isetan Department Store. She stood waiting for the lights to change, unaware of his presence behind her, gazing at the nape of her neck. The thought of this woman, who would be his within a few hours, standing just in front of him gave him mixed feelings of joy and secret sensuality. He identified himself with a hero in a fairy story clad in a mantle of invisibility. The north wind blew in his face, foretelling winter, and old newspapers and fallen leaves whirled in the air. All around, people hurried about their business, their collars turned up against the cold.

At first, it seemed as if the woman was bound for the station, but then she stopped in front of the Meigaza Cinema and gazed at a poster of an old French film that was showing. He stood in the window of the bookshop next door and watched her. The bell signifying the start of the last performance began to ring, and as if this made up her mind for her, the woman went in, just as Ichiro's sixth sense had told him she would. Despite her telling her companions that she had somewhere else to go, she was just another of his victims starving for love. All he need do would be to set a little snare, and she would be his.

For this aging spinster had undoubtedly been upset by the topic of her colleague's marriage, drinking the stale blood of her own missed romance. All he would have to do would be to talk to her and to listen to whatever she had to say. That would be all.

After her back vanished into the entrance, he counted five slowly and then followed her up the steps. He paused to let her get far enough ahead for him to overtake her on the staircase. If no one else interfered, it would be easy.

He steadied his breathing and then began to trot up the steep, narrow stairway to the fifth floor, taking the stairs two at a time.

3

Fusako Aikawa, an English-language typist at the Sato Trading Company, was quite unaware of the fact that Ichiro Honda was pursuing her up the stairs of the Meigaza. She was thinking back to her college days, when she had been a regular frequenter of this cinema. In those days, the five-floor climb had not worried her one little bit. Indeed, it had given her pleasure to climb the stairs in those days, for she had believed that an enchanting world of mystery awaited her at the top; that once there, she would be wafted away to a land of real life. How she had pined for real life in those innocent days, she thought. And when she had got it, what had it turned out to be? What had the last ten years brought her other than going to work and then going home to sleep every evening?

Of course, she had had one or two relationships with men, but what had they signified? They had been no more than boring love affairs—not the real life that she craved, the life of the silver screen. She put them out of her mind. And so she had developed into a trusted, long-service employee who saved half her salary every month, a confirmed old maid who turned up her nose at pleasure. Even she herself did not know at what point she had finally become like that.

What had made her an old maid? Her alarm clock every morning; the crowded trains commuting to work; the monotonous repetitions of the menus at the office cafeteria.

What was more, she was angry with herself for escaping with a spurious excuse from the other girls in the music shop, just running away from the painful topic of her colleague's wedding. Why had she had to pretend that she had another engagement? Why such an obvious lie? Why not tell them that their sentimental chatter disgusted her?

She stopped halfway up the stairs to catch her breath. The bell stopped; in the cinema, the lights would be going down, and she felt as if she was trapped in a vacuum. And then she heard Ichiro Honda's footsteps pounding on the staircase. She stepped to one side to let the stranger pass.

That was not Honda's idea at all, of course, and he cannoned into her, thereby giving himself the chance to talk to her. She slipped and nearly fell, supporting herself against the wall. She turned to glare at him, but was disarmed by the halting Japanese of his apology: "So sorr-eee." It made her smile. He extended a helping hand.

"No, I'm quite all right, really." Little did she understand the hunter's technique. To the contrary, she formed, as she was intended to, a good first impression of this young man with a sporty hat and his tie twisted a little to one side.

"Is cinema more further?" came the deep, attractive voice.

"Yes, a bit." For some reason, perhaps because she was talking to a foreigner, Fusako also adopted a peculiar accent, but this, in a strange way, relaxed her and made her lower

45

her usual guard against unknown men. Somehow, this collision halfway up the stairs with a stranger who spoke broken Japanese seemed a most natural event. She went on:

"It's inconvenient not having an elevator, isn't it?" and set off again up the stairs with him at her side. It never crossed her mind that he was not a foreigner. Even though his features looked rather Japanese, somehow his manner was quite different from that of the men at her workplace. The way he held himself and moved, his special brand of sweet openness, made him clearly a foreigner. She had already stepped into Ichiro's trap.

"This film my country."

He pronounced each word with careful slowness, making sure she could grasp his meaning. As if to answer her unspoken question, he said, "Why I want to see."

"Are you from France?"

"No. Algeria. My name Sobra. I come Japan to study."

The thought of a student from a developing country made Fusako feel protective.

"Oh. I see. This film is set in Algeria, then. Do you still have the Foreign Legion?" She made conversation as they climbed the steps together, and for some reason her heart began to sing.

When they got to the top, the ticket office was closed. Ichiro shrugged his shoulders, and the sight of this so-foreign gesture melted her heart. A girl on the other side of the room called her over to the place where tickets were now being sold, and so she ended up paying for both of them. He

46

argued a bit, but as the newsreel had just started they hurried into the theater.

During the two hours that the film was being screened, he sat bolt upright, his eyes never straying from the screen. He did nothing menacing or suggestive, such as trying to take her hand. In the presence of this quiet foreign student, she felt more and more at ease, and her feelings toward him became warmer.

The film ended, and they left by the emergency staircase at the back. Borne along by the crowd, they found themselves in a narrow back street where there was a jumble of small bars and dustbins. Just like the Casbah, she thought, her mind still on the film. Was the man walking beside her born in a place like this? The very thought made her feel romantic. On the spur of the moment, she said, "Shall we have a drink?"

He accepted, and they went into a bar. Instead of a sweet cocktail, she ordered a highball. She felt quite capable of holding her drink tonight, and in any case she was determined to see this adventure through to the end.

When they left, the man paid.

"Let me stand you one this time," she said, and led the way into another bar. She felt rather proud at having a foreigner in tow, quite apart from which such travelers should be treated with hospitality. Also, she wanted to eat something.

Bit by bit she became a little drunk, and the alcohol made her talkative. She began to tell him everything—about her work, the other people there, the story of her background and childhood, the apartment in Koenji where she lived alone. He asked no questions, but she kept talking. All the things bottled up inside her came out; if he did not fully understand, then so much the better. He just sat and listened, looking at her and smiling, never losing his smile. He was an ideal listener, and so she kept on talking.

She had not realized that the bar was one that stayed open all night, so it was with a sense of shock that she realized that it was already 2 A.M. She had to go home. She stood up unsteadily and nearly fell. As she was recovering, the man paid the bill. Drunk as she now was, she felt loath to part with the foreigner. She clung to his arm; she seemed to be floating, though her heels kept catching on the pavement. She had never been like this before. Half regretfully, she began to coquet him.

"You have nowhere to go tonight, have you?" He shook his head. This childish response reminded her of a stray dog. She stopped a taxi.

"Get in. We'll go to my apartment. I have never taken anyone there before, but you are an exception." She tried to whisper, but her voice came out loud and drunken.

When the taxi reached her apartment, the familiar streetlights at the crossing and even the potted palm at the entrance danced before her eyes like ghosts. For a moment, she could not recognize it and thought that she had come to the wrong place.

At last, though ten years too late, the cinematic real life of which she had dreamed when she was twenty was beginning

48

to happen to her. She unsteadily climbed the uneven steps; the paint was peeling off the plaster. The man was supporting her with one arm; she leaned against him and felt his hand on her breast through the thick overcoat.

She unlocked the door and staggered in. He was still holding her. There was no fire, and the apartment was as cold as ice. She switched on a small foot warmer and sat him beside it while she busied herself making a cup of tea. He got up and stood awkwardly; what an inexperienced young man he seemed! She took two mattresses from the cupboard, two bed covers, clean sheets, and pillowcases and made up the beds. She was rationalizing all the while—nothing to be ashamed of in sleeping quietly next to a man, and anyway she would stay up all night. She called him over.

"Bring the foot warmer. It'll keep you warm; Japan is much colder than your country." What less could she offer a young man from a faraway land of deserts?

The man stood gazing at her with burning eyes. "If he desires me," she thought drunkenly, "do I give him everything?" He began to undress slowly, and she went to take his clothes, only to be seized in a tight embrace. How strong his arms were, even though he looked so quiet! Algerians were certainly different. For a moment she felt afraid and struggled, but then he kissed her. They fell onto the bed, and her struggling stopped. She gave herself to him.

The man took a long time, seeming to taste all of her body. Was this the Algerian way? This put her off for a moment, but the aversion faded away, turning to joy as she felt his lips crawl all over her body. She smelled his sweat; it seemed redolent of the deserts of North Africa that she had seen in the film a few hours before. She was carried to a primitive land, became an animal, and submitted.

4

At about five in the morning, Ichiro Honda turned in the bed and touched the naked woman. She slept on, but he awoke.

For a moment he could not remember where he was, but then he realized that he was in the woman's apartment and not in his bed in the hotel. He raised his left hand in front of his eyes and looked at his self-winding Omega. The date had changed; tomorrow already, he thought. Being careful not to awaken the sleeping woman at his side, he slipped out from under the coverlet.

The icy air hit his naked body, raising goose pimples. He rubbed his chest and powerful shoulders vigorously and quickly dressed. A small light was still burning by the bed, and he looked around the room. There was a portable type-writer on the desk; he thought for a while and then slipped a piece of paper into it and began to type slowly. He kept looking at the woman to see if the rattle of the keys awoke her, but she slept on. He could just see her face above the coverlet; even in sleep she seemed exhausted. Not even the chatter of the typewriter could awaken her. He left the paper in the typewriter and slipped out of the room and into the hall outside, where he was overcome by the sour smell of the apartment. To him it suggested the melancholy of strange places, evoking a sensation he had had many years before in someone's flat in Chicago. He stepped into the street and breathed deeply of the fresh morning air, tasting a refreshing sense of release from the adventure of the night before, but this sensation did not last for long. By the time he had reached the broad thoroughfare of Olympic Street after feeling his way along the misty lane, it was gone.

He hailed a cab, took it to the Meikei-so, where he changed his clothes, and arrived back at the hotel at about 6 A.M. The clerk at the front desk suppressed his curiosity and pretended not to look at him as he handed over the key. Honda thanked him curtly and went upstairs.

All day long, as he tried to get on with his work, Honda sensed a postcoital lassitude that lingered in his body like the dregs of a good wine. He felt too exhausted to go out in the evening and stayed in the hotel. After dinner, he sat on a sofa by the wall in the lobby reading a newspaper in a heavy binder. Idly, he cast his eye over the local news section, when suddenly one item leaped out of the page and caught his eye. He read it carefully; at 2 A.M. on the previous night, it said, a cashier at a supermarket who lived alone had been strangled in her apartment at Kinshibori. The name and address seemed familiar. It seemed to be the same as one of his recent victims, a girl whom he had picked up about two months ago at a dance hall in Koto Rakutenchi.

He lay back and gazed up at the ceiling, his brows furrowed in thought. The cheap apartment in a district full of lumber wholesalers came back to his mind. A foreigner passed by close in front of him striding long and heavily, followed at a trot by a page carrying his suitcase. This brought Honda out of his reverie, and he replaced the newspaper in its rack and walked out of the hotel. He made his way to the newsstand at the underground station and bought every evening edition that he could find. In the train, he avidly read every article concerning the murder of the cashier.

The photographs of the girl certainly looked different from the face that he remembered. The girl he had met, if he recollected aright, had a puffiness around her eyes and cheeks that did not show up in the newspaper photos. Perhaps it wasn't the same girl, but he had to know. He would not relax until he had checked the name and address in his Huntsman's Log.

Getting off the crowded car at Yotsuya Sanchome Station proved difficult; he had to push his way through the throng, and in doing so he felt the body of a young woman press against his thick overcoat. This unconsummated experience appealed to his sensuality. At last he forced his way out onto the empty platform, where he was overcome by a deep sense of unquiet, for it seemed as if everyone remaining in the train was gazing at him accusingly and might set off in pursuit of him at any moment.

He thrust the papers into his pocket and made his way out of the station. On the way to his flat, he stopped off at a small liquor store, which was just closing, and bought a bottle of whiskey and a jar of olives. As soon as he got in, he opened the lid and gulped down a few of the olives; their oil lined his throat and stomach, and he chased them with a whiskey before opening his diary. The name and address were the same; he began to read the passage that he had written two months ago.

September 2
Cloudy
Had business in Chiba in the morning. Came back at 3 P.M.

Toll road congested, so used Chiba Kaido.

Landscape pale gray—soot, smoke, and ashes from the factories lining the road.

Left car at office and walked around Koto Rakutenchi.

Cinemas, gaudy posters for low-class dramas, workmen wearing clogs, tango music played by second-rate orchestras. Heard fragments of music from a dance hall and went in.

Had to buy a ticket for a soft drink in order to gain admission. Floor small and very dark. Looked into tearoom just inside door; a few potential targets in there. But also young men looking like punks or incipient gangsters.

Sat down on my own for a while. Then a woman's voice behind me offered to change my ticket for a soft drink. White pants, blue sweater, looked like she was up to no good, but seemed to be open-minded enough. Talked. Overfamiliar, and a bit vulgar, but she would do.

Today her day off; says she works at a supermarket. Danced a bit and then she offered to take me out to the F Health Center. Was curious, so went. My role today was American buyer of part-Japanese descent. Took a cab to Funabashi. Health center full of women and old people—looked like farmers. All having great time going up on stage and dancing between eating and drinking.

Victim suggested we take a bath together. Had to wait an hour for small bathroom to fall vacant; passed time drinking beer and eating not very good sushi. Maybe because it was still early, but felt out of place amongst all these villagers. She kept talking and I listened, trying to work up desire by looking at the nape of her neck and her alcohol-flushed face. Bathroom free at last. Tipped middle-aged woman in charge, got key, and in we went. Sank into mineral-spring water and looked at victim's body. White flesh seemed to sway under water. Bath was tiled. Touched her body—no adverse response. Sitting in bathtub having fun and feeling desire rising in me. Her breasts and fat bottom caked with the mineral salts; left a taste on my tongue.

Mark of the tiles on her back; reminded me at first of whipping, then of iron-barred windows.

Buzzer rang; time up. Woman in charge of bath looked at us curiously on way out.

Went straight to Kinshicho. Desire aroused and then interrupted—annoying, but perhaps better than the hollow feeling I always get after the act.

Took her to Korean restaurant. She had an enormous appetite—wolfed down a large bowl of rice with nothing but pickles to go with it. Nothing doing tonight, it seemed, but she gave me a map of her apartment and I promised to call around in a few days.

The diary for September 2 ended there, with the sketch map that the girl had drawn attached by tape at the bottom of the page. It was drawn and lettered in a childish hand; he looked absentmindedly at the various landmarks—a tram stop, a moat, a concrete bridge. Gradually the image of the apartment came back to him, and he could clearly remember the bridge, the narrow streets.

The apartment was behind a lumberyard; when he had made his way there, night had drawn its gloomy curtains around him, and he remembered passing by the dark shadows that were bundles of timber.

He thought back to the newspaper reports of the murder. She had been discovered by a middle-school student delivering milk at 5:30 A.M. on that very morning, just when he had been standing on Olympic Street waiting for a taxi. He imagined the boy passing the lumberyard, the milk bottles rattling in the carrier on his bicycle. When he crossed the small garden at the back of her apartment, he had noticed that the window was half-open, and he could see the whole room reflected in the mirror on her dressing table. The woman whom he had seen writhing on the tiles of the bathroom—now the milkboy saw those same limbs writhing, but frozen by death.

Honda remembered that dressing table well. It had been covered with a red square of fine silk, on which were arrayed jars of powder and bottles of cheap creams and lotions. It was now unpleasant to remember that the girl had taken a bottle of milky lotion from that same dressing table and poured it over his body. He threw down the diary in disgust and opened the window, gulping down the cold night air. It was unbelievable that the woman who had innocently pressed her lips all over his body was now dead.

At all events, it was clearly the same woman; the name and address in the diary told him that.

The newspapers reported that on the night of her death a man had visited her room, and that the evidence suggested that he had had sex with her. Kimiko Tsuda must have been something close to a prostitute, he imagined. Although he had no direct evidence as to this—she hadn't asked him for payment—it seemed likely from her overfriendly manner and also from her obvious sexual expertise. Why, she had had a man with her last night . . . and that had been the end of her.

The newspapers also reported that she had had many male friends, so in due course every one of them would be investigated. What about him? No need to worry, surely. He had only been to her room once, and she had only known him as Sobra, a buyer from the U.S.A.

He closed the window, and in that instant, inexplicably, he remembered how large the whites of her eyes had been when she had raised her head from his loins. . . .

At the time, there seemed to be no connection between the murder of his former victim and the fact that he had been sleeping with a new girlfriend at the time.

The connection only became clear much later.

The Second Victim (December 19)

*The Day When Fusako Aikawa Was Strangled at
Akebono-so Apartment at XX, Koenji,
Suginami-ku*

1

At 8 P.M. on the nineteenth of December, Ichiro Honda was
high above Tokyo on the observation platform of Tokyo
Tower. He was accompanied by a girl, a student at an art
school, whom he had met about a week before.

He was wearing a trilby, tipped back slightly, and the buttons of his overcoat were undone. Throughout the proceedings, he kept his hands thrust deeply into his pockets. He
was posing as a correspondent of *The Times* of London. This
was his third meeting with the girl, Mitsuko Kosugi, for he
reckoned she would be a tough nut to crack and was taking
his time over her. However, he had to be back in Osaka by
Christmas Eve, and so tonight it was now or never; he must
shoot at all costs. He therefore kept looking at her out of the
corner of his eye, working out how best to proceed.

Mitsuko was looking out over the nighttime city, which
seemed to be hung with jewels. Her eyes were sparkling; she
wore no makeup and her face was blemished in places. Her
face was thus somewhat unrefined, but by contrast her body

57

was marvelously mature; there was a green, hard unripeness about her that appealed greatly to Honda. She was only nineteen; it was some time since he had enjoyed a woman so young, and he was determined not to let her escape.

He had met her at the Western Art Museum at Ueno, where she was sketching a muscular male statue. It was Ichiro's custom to visit museums two or three times a month, as he found them fruitful hunting grounds. He admired her work and then introduced himself to her as a foreign correspondent. They went to the museum tearoom together, where he drank his tea and ate his cake in a clumsy foreign manner, and he discovered that she was on a long vacation and so was able to persuade her to show him around Tokyo. She agreed, and on the next day she had taken him, not to the famous historical sites or scenic areas, but to the Kabuki theater and on a bus tour around cabarets in Yoshiwara and Akasaka. Tonight they had eaten mudfish and were now visiting Tokyo Tower.

He listened raptly to her explanations, but at the same time could not help staring at the pretty conductress when they went on the bus tour. She had a full bosom and pert buttocks; he didn't mind at all that the conductress was conscious of his gaze. At the Kabuki theater, he tested Mitsuko's reaction by resting his hand on her knee. She ignored the action, fixing her attention on the stage. Was this her way? he wondered. To pretend that nothing was happening, however much a man took advantage of her body? The thought tantalized him.

And then, suddenly, he had tensed and muttered "Disgraceful!" in English.

"What is it?" she asked, gazing anxiously into his face.

"Oh, nothing," he replied in genuine embarrassment. The reality was that the memory came back to him suddenly of a theater in America where he had lusted for a white woman in black tights. Why did this memory suddenly strike him in the Kabuki theater? And what had come over him to yearn for that white woman—too ascetic a life during his studies, perhaps? But wasn't it, after all, natural to entertain such desires at that age? Of course it was, he thought, and calmed down. Why remember a thing like that now? He smiled reassuringly at her.

"Nothing," he repeated.

A little later, he got his hand on her knee again. He had slid his hand a little way up her thigh, relishing the sensation of unfulfillable lust. . . .

And now here they were on Tokyo Tower, and the group of schoolgirls over there had finished with the telescope and they could use it. The girls walked off, speaking in some provincial accent, and he led Mitsuko to the telescope. There was nobody else around.

"Care to have a look?" he asked, putting his hand in his pocket and taking out a coin.

"Oh, yes! I wonder what we'll see!" She ran to the telescope, and Ichiro followed her and slipped in a coin. He put his hand on her shoulder and brought his face close to hers as if to share the viewing with her. Her faint shudder as she

became aware of his hand on her body gave him a thrill.
Three minutes passed, and with a click the lens was closed.
He placed his lips on her cheek, and she did not move. He
twisted his head, trying to find her lips with his, and she nei-
ther resisted nor collaborated. And then, suddenly, out of
the corner of his eye, he detected a movement. Was someone
watching them?

He froze his posture and watched. It seemed that the
movement had come from behind an illuminated tank full
of tropical fish. But if someone was watching, they must
have realized that he had seen them and withdrawn into the
stairway behind, for all he could see now were the fish
swimming under their mercury light.

He kissed the girl, still keeping careful surveillance on the
fish tank, but there was now no sign of anyone there. Perhaps it had been some high school boy. He felt embarrassed
and withdrew, leaving Mitsuko gulping air, the saliva showing in her mouth. He kissed her again, and his attention
wandered from the fish tank and concentrated on the sensa-
tions at the tip of his exploring tongue. There was another
movement, but it was just another couple like them looking
for somewhere to be private together. He clasped Mitsuko
more firmly and kissed her again.

On the way down, the lift was full of country people. Just
as the doors closed, he once again had the sensation of being
watched, but he could see no one.

They hailed a taxi at the entrance. He sat close to her and
put his arm around her and kissed her furtively, but was in-

terrupted by a taxi, which came up close behind them and stayed there, its lights flooding the back of his cab, forcing him to desist lest they be noticed.

They went to a bar, and then to a beer hall. In the noisy beer hall, several drunks peered at them curiously, and they moved on. They went to Shinjuku, to another bar, and then to a sushi shop, by which time he had forgotten all about his feeling of being shadowed at Tokyo Tower—indeed, he was already three parts drunk, and she was beginning to show signs of the alcohol. She did not usually drink much, but to-night he pressed drinks on her, and she proved to have a stronger head than he had. It was already 1 A.M., and he felt unsteady on his feet.

"Let's go to a hotel," he said.

But, to his surprise, she resisted his invitation firmly. So he called a taxi and told it to take them to Asagaya, the area of Mitsuko's apartment. At that, she seemed to relax, and snuggled up to him in the back of the car. Perhaps, after all, he would get a shot at her; perhaps she would invite him back to her apartment.

And so it turned out. When the taxi dropped them, she asked, "Like to come in for a bit?"

He followed her down the narrow alleyway, with stepping-stones set in the dirt. Her flat was in a two-story building second from the entrance to the alley.

"Sorry—you have to take off your shoes. It's a Japanese house," she said to the *Times* journalist.

There was a large shoe cupboard in the entrance hall, with

separate compartments for each of the occupants—some thirty in all, it seemed. She opened the compartment marked "Kosugi" and gave him a pair of slippers.

"This is how my name is written. This character means 'small,' and this one 'cedar.' Interesting, isn't it, our way of writing."

Ichiro Honda nodded and gazed in a fascinated manner at all the names, playing the role of a foreigner fascinated by the Japanese characters. The names were written in a variety of ways, some on grubby slips of paper, one with a large ink-blot half obscuring the name. He ran his finger down the row as she explained the meaning of each name to him. His finger came to rest on the newest nametag of all.

"Obana. 'Little tail.' Funny name, isn't it? She's new here. Room 209—now, whose place did she take, I wonder?"

There was something familiar about this to Honda, and he thought hard as he went up the stairs but couldn't bring it to mind. He completely forgot, in his fuddled state, that this was the name of the key-punch operator who had committed suicide.

The staircase, the hall downstairs, and the landing upstairs were all very spacious, as befitted a building that had formerly been a hospital. Where the reception counter had been, just under the staircase, there was a public telephone.

Mitsuko's room was in the far corner of the ground floor. It was just over one hundred feet square and had a small sink and a gas ring. There was an unfinished painting on an easel and several finished ones stacked against the wall. These he proceeded to examine as Mitsuko boiled the kettle and made instant coffee. They drank the coffee; he was at a loss what to do next, and fiddled with books and a paperknife on the table, and picked up a plaster figure and examined it, pretending he didn't know what to do with his hands, awaiting his chance. Looking at her, he detected increasing anxiety in her eyes.

This was the chance he had been waiting for. She seemed to sense his feeling, for she opened her mouth to speak.

"You are ..." She broke off, perhaps feeling that he would not understand her meaning. He reached out and touched her knee; she pushed him away, but this only served to inflame his desire and he pounced on her, pushing her down onto the floor, and thrust toward her with his hands and his lips. She resisted him fiercely and did not give in.

After thirty minutes of struggle, he gave up. He could not think that this was happening to him ... why? He separated from her and gazed at her face.

"I am sorry. I am just not in the mood today," she said. She pulled down her skirt, which had ridden up in the struggle. There were tears in her eyes.

Ichiro made up his mind to go. He stood up and went to the door. On the way out, he turned and asked her, "Have you got another boyfriend?"

"Oh, no," she said. "Really I haven't."

He smiled wordlessly, went back into the room and kissed her proffered mouth with his dry lips. It was no less than his duty to do so. This woman had become a different creature from the one who had yielded to his kisses, her whole body trembling, at the Tokyo Tower a few hours before. Now he saw her for what she was: dull, a woman lost in daydreams about true love, egoistical, ignorant, nothing.

"Your telephone number, please," he commanded, and she wrote it down in large letters, telling him to call before 10 P.M. and, when the receptionist answered, to give her room number. She rose to see him off, but he pushed her down and made his way out on his own.

Leaving the building, he looked back, but there was not a light to be seen. It seemed that no one else was up at this late hour. He reached the highway and began to walk in the direction of Shinjuku, turning up his coat collar and thrusting his hands into his great coat pockets. Inside, he was raging at his rejection. Suddenly, in a maudlin way, he thought of his wife, patiently enduring her loneliness in Osaka, hundreds of kilometers away. Perhaps it was self-pity, but he thought of his fruitless endeavors to bridge this gap. *It is only because of that—that's why I waste my time hunting women,* he thought for a few seconds, but then he rejected the thought, at which moment a taxi arrived. He got in, and at first told the driver to take him to his apartment in Yotsuya Sanchome, but then suddenly changed his mind and decided to visit Fusako Aikawa, the typist he had met at the cinema. Her apartment was only one stop away on the subway from Mitsuko Kosugi's. He got out of the taxi near her apartment and walked the last few yards. He had no particular pressing desire for a woman now, but needed something to distract his mind from the emptiness he had sensed when walking in the road.

He had difficulty in finding the building, but eventually

reached it, arriving in the front yard, which was muddied by an overflow of sewage. In the dim light he saw some underwear on the clothesline, which someone had forgotten to take in. The garments floated like white ghosts in the dark.

Inside, the staircase awaited him, its vast maw ready to swallow him as he climbed.

2

Hesitantly, he knocked gently on Fusako Aikawa's door, but there was no reply. Last time he had left her sleeping with the hem of her satin negligee riding up over her breasts; the lascivious image floated back into his mind. How bewitching she had looked! He pressed his ear close to the door and listened. Within, all was silent.

So far, he had visited this apartment three times; on the first occasion, Fusako had taken him there, but subsequently he had visited her without any warning, and she had always been glad to see him, even as late as 1 A.M. "Come whenever it suits you," she had said to the young Algerian student, and he felt in her something protective, which was different from the emotions displayed toward him by his other victims. This gave him a strange sense of security.

He looked at his watch; it was already ten to three. Not wishing to disturb or attract the attention of the neighbors, he knocked again gently, but there was still no reply. It was late; perhaps she was sleeping heavily, he reasoned. He decided to go home, but the same instinct that makes one try the door of an empty house took hold of him and he turned the knob. The door was unlocked, and he stepped into the room.

There was a strange, sweet smell inside, something stagnant, reminiscent of Formalin in a hospital, both sweet and sour at the same time. He turned on the light, and saw Fusako spread-eagled on the bed, stark naked, her legs slightly apart, her hands resting at her sides. Her head was turned to one side. Could she be sleeping naked in this cold weather?

He moved over and stood by her. Her face was swollen and tinged with a purplish hue, and there was a red line about her throat, about as thick as a belt. It looked as if she had been strangled. He moved his hand toward her fat underbelly, so pink, and for a moment he imagined that she was breathing. Could she really be dead? But there was no doubt that she was.

He stepped back sharply, but at the same time as he felt terror he also felt drawn toward her by carnal desire. He hurried out of the room, switching off the light and obliterating the sight of that naked body. Creeping down the staircase, he realized that he had had a momentary desire to rape Fusako's corpse, and knew that he could have been capable of such a cold-blooded act.

But still, he thought, who on earth could have forced Fusako Aikawa into such a posture? What other man had she let into her room? He felt as if the dead woman had betrayed him somehow. But he had no idea that Fusako's death was another step on the path to his own misfortune.

*   *   *

He walked away from the apartment rapidly and met no one for several minutes. Then he came to a well-lit intersection and found a policeman standing there. They exchanged glances, but Ichiro said nothing, and the policeman merely tapped his left palm twice with the flashlight he was carrying in his right hand and then moved on without a word. Honda had no intention of reporting the murder that he had discovered.

He caught a taxi on Olympic Street and, his deep voice full of depression, told it to take him to Yotsuya Sanchome. Sitting in the back of the speeding cab, it suddenly occurred to him that the murder of Fusako Aikawa bore a similarity to the killing of the supermarket cashier about two months before. She, too, had been strangled at night, although in her case they had found the string of her Japanese nightgown around her neck. And the coincidence went further; on the night that Kimiko Tsuda was murdered in Kinshicho, had he not had sex with Fusako for the first time? And tonight, had he not expected to enjoy Mitsuko Kosugi—this very night upon which Fusako had been murdered? He felt an awful sense of premonition, but kept it at bay by muttering "No! No!" to himself several times. After all, his visit to Fusako's room had been but a sudden whim. If he had not tried the door, then he would have left totally unaware of what had happened. So therefore the death of Fusako had nothing to do with him, he reasoned. But in the back of his mind, he heard a voice whispering doubts: "Do you really believe that? Did Fusako Aikawa's death really have nothing to do with you?" And the voice would not be stilled.

The taxi stopped outside his secret flat, and Honda absentmindedly handed the driver a five-hundred-yen bill and told him to keep the change. The driver, a good-natured-looking old man, took off his cap and bowed his profuse thanks. As he did so, he memorized the face of this unusual customer who had tipped him twice the fare. Another witness had unwittingly been created to Honda's future disadvantage.

He entered the Meikei-so and lay down on the bed without taking off his clothes; putting his hands behind his neck, he stared at the ceiling, a vacant look in his black-ringed eyes. How could such a thing happen to him? So far, his secret life of fishing for women had gone without a hitch. But surely it was nothing—merely a coincidence? He strove to drive the doubts from his mind, but without success. A new, dark thought began to obsess him—both of the women were his victims, were they not? Both had had sexual relations with him. And as he moved on to each fresh victim, a murder was committed. Was this some epidemic—was there a carrier stalking the town? He loosened his tie, undid his shirt buttons and massaged his chest. Was he a leper, his body gradually rotting away? But the feel of his muscular, hairy chest reassured him.

But then: *What if all the women I touch are murdered?* Surely this was impossible. What had happened so far was mere chance. It was arbitrary that two women with whom he had slept were now dead—there could be no possible connection. It was all chance.

Sluggishly, he pulled himself up off the bed and changed his suit and prepared to go back to the hotel. In his mind rang that one word, his breastplate: "Chance."

3

All day long Ichiro Honda waited with mounting impatience for the evening papers to come out, expecting to read of the discovery of Fusako Aikawa's dead body. In his office on the sixth floor, he listened to the 3 P.M. news, but there was nothing on it. Whereas at the time of the last murder he had stayed fairly calm, this time he couldn't—perhaps because he had seen the corpse with his own eyes.

He switched off the radio, got up, and went to the window. On the road far below, cars were moving like toys and pedestrians like ants; it was impossible to tell the difference between men and women from this height. He thought of how, amongst the billions of people on earth, only two knew that, in a flat with the plaster peeling in Koenji, a woman's body was beginning to decay: only two people—himself and the murderer who had strangled her with a nylon stocking. He felt a weird sense of affinity for the murderer, as if they were partners in crime. There was some poem like that, wasn't there? He couldn't remember. He went out to buy the early editions of the evening papers.

In the corridor, he met an acquaintance from the General Affairs Department. He wore rimless spectacles and spoke with an effeminate voice.

"When are you next off to Osaka, then?"

"The day after tomorrow. I always at least spend Christmas with my wife."

"Do give your father-in-law my best regards."

During this exchange, he beamed and looked at ease, but as soon as the other man was gone his face resumed its look of gravity and exhaustion.

He bought several evening papers, but there was no news in any of them of the death of Fusako Aikawa.

When work was over, he walked down Ginza, occupying himself by staring at displays of women's shoes or else by standing behind a girl who was trying on scarves. Reaching Shinbashi, he went into a large pachinko hall, which had previously been a cabaret. The staircase and the ceiling were all too gorgeous for a pinball parlor, he thought. He looked around; the players, each riveted to his machine, seemed to lose themselves in the oppressive clamor. Perhaps he could, too; he bought a hundred yen worth of balls and sat down at the nearest vacant machine. As he played, he noticed a girl of about fifteen peering around the machine at him. She had single-lidded eyes heavily painted with mascara and seemed to display an interest in him. For his part, he was getting bored with the monotony of the game; his saucer was full of balls and emitted an oily smell. He noticed a man of his own age standing behind him.

"Care to try?" he said.

The man, despite his cheap suit, had his pride. He flushed at what he took to be an insult. Honda ignored him and walked out, leaving the balls behind him.

The murder was not reported on that day, nor indeed the next day, finally appearing in the evening papers of the third day. Now that it at last came out, it was a shock to him. He bought all the evening papers and took the underground to his hideout in Yotsuya Sanchome. He was tightly squeezed between other passengers and closed his eyes, listening to the rattle of the wheels over the points. The headline he had read kept appearing in front of him.

SOBRA, AN ALLEGED ALGERIAN, KEY WITNESS

As he visualized this, he could almost smell the newsprint.

When he got to his apartment, he started to devour the newspapers eagerly. Perhaps because he had seen the corpse, he felt a far deeper interest than he had in the case of the cashier. Again and again it came up: "Sobra an important witness."

However, only one paper, and that a second-rate one, saw any connection between the two crimes. He got out the two-month-old papers that had reported the last murder and, blowing the dust off them, sat down and began to compare the two cases.

There were four similarities.

Firstly, both women had been strangled.

Secondly, the victims were single women living alone.

Thirdly, both seemed to have intimate male friends.

These were the obvious points in common. In both cases, the papers had suggested a degree of intimacy between the killer and his victim as there were no signs of resistance, but otherwise there was nothing of interest.

And there was a fourth similarity that only he knew

about. Both of the victims featured in his hunting log. This fact, unknown to everyone else, was the only thing that bound him to the cases. And what could he do about it? Nothing.

Events had to develop as they would. He was due to fly back to Osaka by the night plane; for a few days, at least, his hunting would cease.

And with this comforting thought, he dozed off.

The Third Victim (January 15)

*The Day When Mitsuko Kosugi Was Strangled at
Midori-so at XX Asagaya, Suginami-ku*

I

Ichiro Honda flew back to Osaka on Christmas Eve. He had
taken leave over the whole Christmas and New Year season.
At the airport, he got a splinter in his hand from a temporary plywood partition that had been put up alongside the
walkway, and it drew blood. He mopped the blood with his
handkerchief but did not bother to ask the stewardess for io-
dine.

He looked down at the lights of Tokyo. Oh marvelous
living city, that seemed to breathe as he watched it! What
did it matter to him that human beings were dying there,
people being murdered, all the time?

At Itami Airport, his wife met him. "Welcome home,"
she said smilingly. "Have a good flight?" They agreed to go
for a walk down the bustling streets of Shinsaibashi before
dining there. They then visited a bar where Taneko was
known, and it was midnight before they sat down to dinner.
They had reserved a table for two, and as it was now

Christmas Day they followed their custom and ordered turkey and opened a bottle of champagne.

"Do you remember," he said, toasting her, "Christmas Eve in New York?"

"Of course," she replied. "We went to Très Bon."

"That's right," he said. Then, changing the subject, "Let's dance."

She was wearing a black, low-necked dress with an orchid pinned to it. She danced closely in his arms, not caring if the flower was crushed or not. They went back to their table.

"Ah, Très Bon," she said wistfully. "We were so green that we didn't know anywhere else. So we went there on New Year's Eve, too."

"So we did."

"And at midnight, when the church bells rang, everyone started kissing each other, even total strangers."

"Yes—very American, wasn't it?"

"Yes, but so lovely. I wish we were back in those times again." She nuzzled close to him, and he felt her soft hair brush his face, but felt a repugnance beyond his control and turned away quickly. As an excuse he slipped his forefinger down the front of his collar and twisted it around vigorously. "The hotel laundry just doesn't know how to starch a shirt properly," he explained apologetically. His wife withdrew and fell silent. Once again, they were up against the solid, opaque film that always seemed to separate them.

"It can't be helped," he muttered, as he always did on

74

these occasions. His wife remained silent, her eyes showing either reproach or pity, he could not tell which.

After dinner, they went bar-crawling again and had a superficially good time calling strolling musicians, singing songs, and drinking heavily. Before they noticed, it was 3 A.M.; the alcohol seemed to have washed away some of the latent hostility between them.

They decided it would not be safe to drive, so Taneko left her Mercedes Benz in a garage and they walked arm in arm until they caught a taxi and drove back to Ashiya. As they passed through the stone gate, the light in the entrance hall came on, and the old housekeeper appeared like a phantom before them.

"Welcome home, young mistress," she said in her old-fashioned way. She was over seventy and a faithful retainer of the old school; her rheumy eyes were unblinking as she gazed at them attentively. Ichiro found this old woman, who had played a mother's role to Taneko and still seemed to do so, difficult to handle. She had used exactly the same stilted greeting when they came back from America as she did tonight.

"You shouldn't have waited up for us!" protested Taneko. But the housekeeper ignored her, concentrating on locking the door.

They looked into the dining room to make sure that Taneko's father wasn't still up and then made their way upstairs to their bedroom.

Ichiro took a shower and came out to find his wife removing her makeup. She looked at him and said in a matter-of-fact way, "Darling, you kept repeating Hamlet's line in the bar. You know, 'To be or not to be.' What did you mean by that?"

Ichiro looked at her in the mirror; by now, she was combing her long, black hair.

"Nothing in particular," he replied. "I just think of death from time to time nowadays, that's all." His wet hair hung down his forehead, contrasting blackly with his face as pale as a corpse, but there was a strange beauty about his face nevertheless.

She went on combing her hair; after a little while, she questioned him again in the same expressionless manner. "Why so morbid, all of a sudden?"

"Well, I don't know . . ." He went to turn down the central heating in the bedroom while his wife went into the bathroom. During her absence he lay on his back with his eyes open. She came back, wearing a beige dressing gown.

"Well, after all, we didn't get divorced, did we?" she remarked, taking off the dressing gown and standing naked for a moment before getting into bed. Her body was silhouetted against the bedside lamp and cast a shadow on the ceiling.

Without turning toward her, he replied, "Maybe it's because we're Christians." His voice was so soft that she could hardly hear him.

She turned on her side and examined her husband's profile.

"You know, you are still very important to me. I feel that you are a half of my body," she said.

They fell silent; not even their breathing could be heard in

76

the quiet room. Ichiro suddenly got out of bed, standing on the cold floor, and looked down at his wife, who had closed her eyes. She lay motionless, and he imagined that he could see shadows under her eyelashes. He moved toward her and peeled back the bedclothes, exposing her white body, but still she did not move. He buried his face in her pudenda and lay there gripping her breasts; still she did not move. After a while, he looked up, the expression in his eyes hollow. He placed his hands on her stomach; the skin was soft, but not as soft as the skin of his victims.

He thought of the infant, born obscenely deformed, the birth of which had come between him and his wife. He threw himself down on her, kissing her frantically—her breasts, her narrow waist, her armpits. She moved spasmodically, but her eyes remained closed.

After a while he desisted and began to sob—but was it tears, or was it hysterical laughter brought on by despair? Once again he was impotent in the presence of his wife, as he had been a week ago . . . a fortnight ago . . . a year ago . . . two years ago. . . .

Taneko opened her eyes and gazed at him silently; her look was one to kill any emotion.

He went back to his side of the bed, his hands hanging by his side in the dejection of a defeated fighter.

2

On the fifth of January, he took the noon plane back to Tokyo. Contrary to his normal custom, he had a window seat. The skies were clear and cloudless, and he could see the pure white cone of Mount Fuji from a great distance. Looking at the unsullied mountain against the blue sky, he found it hard to believe that two women had been killed in Tokyo at the end of the last year. The memory of Fusako Aikawa lying naked and dead in the dark, damp room in Koenji had all but vanished from his mind. How foolish he had been to fear that he would be accused of the crime! He had been afraid of the scandal and didn't want to get involved, that was all.

However, he had better stop using the name Sobra from now on. He could change the name on the passport to something a bit more British, something with a grave and serious ring about it. Hume, perhaps, or Wigland; those were good names. Just as other salarymen applied themselves, during their leisure, to do-it-yourself, he would apply himself to modifying the passport.

Well, it was time for a change, and he could alter his life so simply; the obsessive fear of being hunted himself vanished from his mind. He accepted a cup of tea from the stewardess. Next to him, a fat foreigner was engaged in the crossword of an English-language newspaper. He felt cocooned and safe in this environment—the fat foreigner, the smiling stewardess, the passengers all around him. He had nothing to do with the deaths of the two women; it was purely coincidence that they had both been his victims. He really began to believe that he was safe. All he had to do was to abandon the name Sobra, and Ichiro Honda's connection with the murders would be severed. He touched the window and wrote the name "Sobra" on it with his fingertip and then rubbed it out.

There is a game called *capping* or *tailing*—he had heard it called both. One takes the last syllable of a word and starts the next word with the same syllable. Although it is a game for two, he played it with himself to pass the time. He began with the name Sobra and carried on from there. Playing this game of linking suddenly brought another linkage clearly before his mind. Of course he could not be proved guilty; he always had an alibi. The alibis linked onto each other, just as in his game.

For example, whilst the cashier was being murdered in her room at Kinshicho on the fifth of November, he had been with Fusako Aikawa in her flat at Koenji on the other side of Tokyo. Even if he was suspected, apart from the scandal of sleeping with someone not his wife, he was safe; he had an alibi.

And—linking again—while Fusako Aikawa was being murdered, he was with the art student. Admittedly, the two apartments had been much closer than in the previous case, but nonetheless he had certainly been in Asagaya with Mitsuko at the time. So he had a watertight alibi in each case.

Watertight? But wasn't there a fatal flaw?

Fusako Aikawa, his alibi in the cashier's murder, was dead. His alibi in that case was illusory. He looked out of the window, but these ominous feelings destroyed the beauty of the countryside.

If asked where he had been on the night of the cashier's murder, there was no one to support his evidence. Why had he not realized this before? He cursed himself for his foolish complacency.

Viewed in this light, the two murders began to seem closely interwoven. Rather than two separate incidents, he was looking at a sequence of events.

Had Fusako Aikawa been murdered for no other reason than to destroy his alibi? In the back of his head, he heard the mocking voice of the killer. What was the motive? Was he reading too much into it? Who stood to lose most from the death of Kimiko Tsuda?

Someone was trying to frame him.

The circle of his logic complete, he was now convinced that his theory was correct. The two murders had been committed in order to entrap him. He stirred in his seat and groaned; the foreigner looked up from his crossword for a moment, studying him dubiously before returning to his pastime.

And if that was true . . .

Then the murderer would strike again. To destroy his other alibi. By killing Mitsuko Kosugi. She was the last link in the chain.

The in-flight announcement crackled over the loudspeakers, instructing the passengers to fasten their seat belts. Below, he could see the approaches to Haneda Airport. And he still could not understand why someone was trying to trap him.

As soon as he was outside the terminal, he telephoned Mitsuko's apartment at Asagaya. The hoarse voice of the receptionist told him that Mitsuko had gone home to her fam-

ily for the holiday and would not be back before the fifteenth. He replaced the receiver and stood lost in thought
for a while before taking a taxi back to the Toyo Hotel.

3

The narrow lane leading to Mitsuko Kosugi's apartment was
unlit and was bordered by fences weatherproofed with black
tar. It was pitch dark, and visibility was not helped by a
misty drizzle. Ichiro Honda pulled down his waterproof hat,
turned up the collar of his coat, and made his way down the
alley. The stepping-stones were slightly raised above the
black silt, and he had to tread carefully to avoid tripping.

At the entrance, he peered over the fence. He could see a
faint light glowing behind the curtains of Mitsuko's room;
she was in.

Relieved, he opened the front door and went in. He
opened the shoe compartment marked "Kosugi" and slipped
in his low-heeled Guccis. There was a pair of lady's brown
pumps in there already.

He went into the hall. The reception desk was dark and
empty, just as Mitsuko had told him it would be at this
hour. He turned and made his way down the broad corridor
leading to her room.

The corridor turned sharply to the left just before her
door, forming a right angle like a carpenter's square. So once
he stood in front of her door, he was invisible from the rest
of the passage. So nobody would see him or question him.

From some nearby room, he could hear the muffled

sounds of a television program. It was 11:30; someone was watching the midnight show. Upstairs, he could hear footsteps, but apart from these two sounds, the building was silent. He made his way stealthily down the passage.

He reached her door and knocked, at first softly and then louder. There was no reply. He leaned on the door of the broom cupboard opposite her room and thought. Later, he remembered the sign "Broom Cupboard" lettered on the door.

He tried her door, and just as in the case of his visit to the apartment in Koenji, it opened to his touch.

He stepped in and shut the door behind him. Ahead of him was a small sink, and to the left a curtain strung on a wire shut off the main room.

"Are you in?" he called, making his voice falter on purpose. But there was no reply. He began to feel a brooding sense of oppression. His chest felt tight; try as he might, he could not rid himself of the recollection of Fusako Aikawa's death. Would he find Mitsuko Kosugi in there, naked . . . and dead?

He put his hand on the curtain and paused to collect himself. He had a premonition that he was going to find a death within. He pulled the curtain aside forcefully.

There was no one in the room.

But there were signs that someone had been there until a few minutes ago.

He went over and sat down in a swivel chair in front of the desk. He looked around the room. He had phoned her three hours earlier, as soon as she had returned from her holiday, and had suggested that he would meet her at 11:30. He had suggested meeting somewhere outside, but she was plainly overjoyed to receive his phone call and insisted that he come to her room.

"I'll toast—er—special New Year cakes for you." She seemed unsure about making him understand the word *mochi* in English. He could hear her voice now as he observed the rice cakes wrapped in newspaper on the dining table. She must have slipped out to borrow some seasonings, he decided. He lit a cigarette and waited.

Blowing smoke out into that small room, he examined his surroundings. Clearly an art student's room, with its volumes of painters on the bookshelves, the canvases stacked against the wall. The closet was ajar, and he could see a red silk quilt stowed away inside. He had not slept with a woman for a month. Seeing the bedding, he felt his desire surging up within him. He yawned and rotated the chair around to face the other wall. The chair creaked noisily in the silent room.

He was facing a walnut-veneered wardrobe with a mirror on the door. Unconsciously he gazed into the mirror. It reflected back, showing him a face with disordered hair; his complexion seemed stagnant in that dim light. It was not a healthy face.

And then he saw a small length of maroon-colored silk caught in the wardrobe door and hanging down. Without thinking, he fingered his silk tie, which was not his maroon-

83

colored favorite. Was there not something familiar about
the color of that two-inch-long piece of silk? It looked exactly like his favorite tie.

Leadenly, he pushed himself out of the chair and walked
over to the wardrobe. He was in the presence of a mystery
that he must solve. What was his tie doing in Mitsuko Kosugi's room? He reached for the door handle, but his hand
was unsteady and on the first pass he missed.

He was hesitant about prying into someone else's wardrobe without her permission. But, after all, he told himself,
he was only checking—nothing wrong with that.

Perhaps the wardrobe was new; he had difficulty in opening the door until he applied his weight. He pulled hard; the
hinge grated, the door opened, and . . .

The dead body of Mitsuko Kosugi rolled out, leaning on
his body.

By reflex action, he warded her off, pushing her back, feeling the warmth that was still in her flesh. He could smell the
scent of her hair, but more pervasive still was the same scent,
half sweet, half sour, that he had smelled in Fusako Aikawa's
room.

Turning his head aside in horror, he pushed the body back
into the wardrobe and shut the door upon it. His hands were
trembling, his body suffused with a deathly chill; he could
hardly breathe. His body seemed to have solidified where he
stood.

"Oh monstrous! Monstrous!" he groaned. He could still
feel the touch of the woman's inelastic skin under his finger-

tips. He rubbed his hand on his trousers as if to wipe the sensation away.

The corpse was in a kneeling position, the better to fit into the wardrobe, its hands hanging loosely by its sides. And around its throat was his tie! He wanted to scream, but his voice was frozen in his mouth.

He went back to the chair and sat down. His whole body shuddered with fear and anger admixed. What was he to do? He lit a cigarette and reached for the ashtray, the Pavlovian actions of a man deep in thought.

Should he call the police? Or the manager of the apartment? To be involved in such a case would mean social ruin. But if he just ran away, what about the tie of his, knotted about her neck? Whatever else he did he must recover that tie first.

It was hanging in my wardrobe in Yotsuya. Who brought it here? Who tied it around her throat? he thought, the anger welling up within him. And then: *It's deliberate. It's another trap.* How could he escape the jaws of this trap?

He did not stop to think that, the more he tried to escape it, the tighter it would grip him.

He went back to the wardrobe and opened the door. This time, Mitsuko Kosugi's body did not roll out. Her head hung loosely on her neck. Her hands were limp by her side. Her hair was in disarray. It was exactly as it had been when he had pushed her back inside the wardrobe.

Fighting back his nausea, he reached down and loosened the tie, which was biting into her throat. It had been knotted very tightly; as he removed it, he could clearly see the livid marks of strangulation. He folded the tie, put it in his pocket, and shut the wardrobe door on the corpse.

He went over to the door. Before passing through the curtain, he looked back to see that he had forgotten nothing, stepped out, and his hand on the doorknob, looked back again. He could see nothing; he touched his hand to his head, verifying that he was wearing his hat, and, satisfied, turned to open the door.

It wouldn't open!

The blood rushed to his head, and he nearly fainted. But of course it would open; he had walked through that self-same door a few minutes earlier, had he not? It must be stiff. He gripped the handle firmly, twisted it and pushed against the door with all his might. Apart from the creak of a budging screw, there was no reaction.

The door was locked.

He stooped and peered through the keyhole. The naked bulb outside shone on the wall and the door opposite—nothing else. Nobody. He gave up and went back into the room.

"Why is it locked? Why is it locked?" he kept asking himself. He crouched on the floor like a trapped animal overcome by the exhaustion of its struggles. He looked up and saw the window.

That was his route of escape.

Outside, the horn of an automobile sounded, jarring on his nerves. The squeal of brakes, the footsteps upstairs, the drone of the television set, the faint sound of music—all of these seemed to grate upon his nerves. Remote as these sounds were, they seemed to be coming closer. The walls and floor of the room seemed to be closing in on him, and everything all of a sudden became colorless. He must escape!

He moved over to the window and touched the curtain before he realized that he might be seen. He went back and switched off the light, noticing irrelevantly the dust upon its shade. Creeping through the darkness, he opened the window.

There was nobody outside.

He climbed out in his stocking feet and carefully closed the window, taking care to make no noise. He felt the damp and slippery ground chilling the soles of his feet.

He went around to the entrance, peeped inside and opened the door stealthily. He made sure that he was unobserved and then opened the shoe box marked "Kosugi." He reached inside.

His shoes were gone!

He was absolutely certain that he had put them in that box. What on earth could have happened? He fumbled inside; the pumps were still there, but not his shoes. Fear ran up and down his spine as he feverishly opened the boxes above and below and on either side. But his shoes were nowhere to be found.

He heard a door open suddenly somewhere on the ground floor and leaped backward. The duckboard slid under his feet, emitting a scratching sound. He forgot about his shoes and ran out into the alleyway, stubbing his toe hard on a stepping-stone as he ran. The pain was agonizing, but he hobbled on as fast as he could, got to the main road and stopped a taxi. Fortunately the driver did not seem to notice that he was shoeless.

He told the man to drive to Yotsuya Sanchome and lay in the back, pressing his forehead against the cool glass of the window. He was overcome with despair. Somewhere in the dark he heard a siren; had they discovered the body already? Had the police been called?

He felt as if he was being pursued and slumped down in the seat. The driver slowed down; the siren came closer and closer, overtaking them with a burst of headlights into the taxi.

"Fire somewhere," said the driver, and Honda looked up and was relieved to see a fire engine and not a police car.

He got off some distance before the Meikei-so. It would not do to have the driver remember his destination; he was becoming cautious.

As a result, he had to walk the hundred yards or so of asphalt road to his apartment in his socks, which became soaking wet. Also, his big toe was throbbing, and the pain made it hard to walk. When he got into his room, he took off the muddy socks, one of them bloodstained, and discovered that he had broken the nail of his toe halfway down. He wrapped his foot in a handkerchief and massaged his toe.

He had to check his tie in the wardrobe. He pulled the tie out of his pocket, looked at it, and hurled it to the ground as if it had turned into a poisonous snake. For there were initials sewn into it, and they were his.

Hoping for the one-in-a-million chance that would prove

him wrong, he went to the wardrobe and opened it. Perhaps his tie was there and this one belonged to someone else with the same initials. . . . He felt a searing pain in his left cheek and sprang back. It felt as if a red-hot skewer had struck him. For a moment he had a blackout, and then he touched his cheek; it was covered with blood. He looked down on the ground; at his feet was a thin blade attached to a length of bamboo. The wardrobe had been booby-trapped.

Ten or so ties swung mockingly on the rail inside the door, but his maroon tie was not amongst them. His eyes filled with tears; the pain and the torment had made a cry-baby out of Don Juan. Pressing his hand to his cheek, he staggered over to the desk. His hunter's diary, which he always kept under a paperweight on the top, was gone!

He lay face down on the bed. When, after a few minutes, he rolled over, for an awful instant he could not see.

4

Early in the morning of January 25, ten days after he had fled Mitsuko Kosugi's room, Ichiro Honda was arrested for murder. The police came to room 305 in the Toyo Hotel and took him away.

The police had been able to trace the man calling himself Sobra through the handmade Italian shoes that had been left at the scene of the crime. They had been a special order, so tracing their owner was a simple matter. This had never occurred to him, nor had he thought in the meantime of going to the police and explaining what had happened.

Since the murder, he had taken no initiative but had just waited to see what would happen. He was like an insect that has lost its wings. About the only thing he did was visit the Meikei-so three days after the murder. He was worried that the taxi driver might have remembered the Meikei-so, but this turned out to be the least of his worries. For when he entered his room, he noticed that someone had taken away the bamboo with the blade in it, which he had put in the corner. This not unnaturally stunned him. But he carried on as he had intended; he packed all his belongings into a bag and informed the manager that he was moving out and wished to settle the balance of the rent.

He roped up the bag, addressed it to his father's house in Kagoshima, and sent it by rail.

Each day on his way to work, he would follow the case in the papers. The police were hunting for Sobra; well and good—they could never identify him as being Sobra. His main fear was that he might somehow come to be embroiled in the case; he feared the resulting scandal. However, he reassured himself that this could not possibly happen.

In the evenings he hardly ever went out anymore. He killed time lying on his bed in his room, waiting for things to blow over. But when he slept, he had nightmares; he dreamed that he was being crushed by heavy weights and woke up shouting and in a cold sweat.

He followed the progress of the investigation as well as he could by buying all the papers and listening to the radio whenever he got the chance. The newspapers reported that the same criminal had been responsible for all of the murders. On about the twenty-third he watched a TV program featuring the officer in charge of the case, a man with thinning hair and a distrustful look in his eyes. Little did he think that within a few days he would be facing this man across the interrogation table. The policeman said that the criminal had left a vital clue on the scene and that his arrest was only a matter of time. Maybe not tomorrow, but the day after, or else the day after that. Tomorrow never comes, thought Honda scornfully.

However, the day came when he was awakened by knocking at his bedroom door and opened it to admit three men, one of them holding a warrant for his arrest. They seized him and handcuffed him like an animal and bundled him into a car.

Seated in the car as it sped toward police headquarters, a policeman on either side gripping him tightly by the arms, he looked back with nostalgia to the morning of the fifth of November when he had been awakened by somebody in slippers walking down the corridor outside. That was the day of the first murder, when his luck had begun to run out. What had become of the beautiful freedom that he had once so enjoyed?

The policemen on either side of him reeked of tinned salmon or of bean-paste soup with spring onions. These homely smells bespoke domestic peace and quiet.

The examination at the police headquarters went on for twenty days, and all he could do was deny that he was guilty. He began to wonder if he was going mad. They refused to allow him to see anyone, even a lawyer. The line that the

police took was not the customary one of urging him to confess. Instead, they thrust more and more irrefutable evidence
before him and asked him how he could possibly deny his
guilt. It was like a psychological torture for him; his only
alibis were worthless, or rather uncallable.

They asked him where he had left his Italian shoes, and
when he said that they had vanished from the shoe box by
the entrance, they laughed and told him that they had
turned up wrapped in newspaper in Mitsuko Kosugi's closet,
and that the only fingerprints on them were his—and her's.

They produced the herringbone jacket, which they had recovered from his father's house. Out of the pockets came the
maroon tie—and a nylon stocking and a key. He remembered the tie, but was not conscious of having had the
stocking used in the murder of Fusako Aikawa or Mitsuko
Kosugi's room key.

He began to think that perhaps, after all, he was guilty,
that he had committed the murders without being conscious
of it.

Furthermore, they told him, although he claimed only to
have been in the rooms of the two murdered women for a
very short time, they had found semen of his blood group in
the bodies of the women. This was evidence suggesting that
he had spent at least long enough there to have had sexual
intercourse with his victims.

A rare blood group, and one that was found in a blood-
stain at one of the scenes of his crimes: AB Rh-negative.
Only one person in two thousand had it—and he was one of
them. He was at a loss for words.

And so he relapsed into silence, saying nothing no matter what they showed him or told him. After he was committed for trial, he sat staring blankly at the prison walls, asking himself again and again, "Who did it? Who did it?"

But then he ceased to ask himself this question, because in his heart of hearts he knew that there was no way to find out the answer to it.

Interval

Ichiro Honda, engineer, aged 29, sentenced to death on June 30 at Tokyo District court on charges of sex-related murders. The defendant denied the charges.

On a charge of murdering Kimiko Tsuda on November the 5th, he was found not guilty on grounds of insufficient evidence.

On a charge of murdering Fusako Aikawa on December the 19th, and on another charge of murdering Mitsuko Kosugi on January the 15th, he was found guilty.

There were no extenuating circumstances in either case.

The verdict was handed down a hundred and fifty-six days after the arrest of the accused at the Toyo Hotel.

The defendant immediately filed notice of appeal to the Tokyo court of appeals, claiming that the verdict was wrong.

Important items of evidence upon which expert witnesses testified:

A pair of low-heeled gentleman's shoes of Italian manufacture, left by the defendant in Mitsuko Kosugi's room.

A maroon-colored tie, the size of which corresponded exactly with the strangulation marks on Mitsuko Kosugi's neck.

A woman's brown stocking, which, it was testified, was of

a size corresponding to the strangulation marks on the neck of Fusako Aikawa.

Transcript of evidence given on the third day of the trial. Examination of expert medical witness by the Public Prosecutor:

Question. Was there any evidence to suggest that the victim, Mitsuko Kosugi, struggled with her assailant?

Answer. The only evidence was the presence of blood under all her fingernails, except her two thumbs and the little finger of her right hand. The blood was deeply engrained under her nails.

Question. Of what type was this blood?

Answer. Type AB, Rh-negative.

Question. Of what type was the victim's blood?

Answer. Type O.

Question. Then you would agree that the blood found under the victim's nails could not have been her own?

Answer. Yes, I agree.

Questions put by the judge to the defendant:

Question. What is your blood type?

Answer. Type AB, Rh-negative.

Question. When did you learn this was your type?

Answer. When I entered Asia Moral University and my blood was tested by the Institute of Biology there.

Question put by the judge to the arresting police officer:

Question. When you examined the defendant after taking him into custody, did you find any scars or other indication of recent injury?

Answer. I had no warrant to carry out a physical examination, so I could not carry out a full check. However, I noticed that there were small scabs on both his left cheek and the back of his right hand.

Summation of points arising from the foregoing evidence made by the judge:

1. Whether or not there were any wounds on the defendant's body, which appear to have been made on about January 15th.

   There were such wounds.

2. The blood type of the defendant.

   Type AB Rh-negative.

3. The blood type evinced in the defendant's semen.

   Secretion type of type AB.

Evidence presented by the prosecution was based upon thirty-five man-days of research. Amongst the witnesses called were:

96

A hotel receptionist.
Gave evidence that on the day of one of the crimes,
Ichiro Honda returned to the hotel in the early morning.

A policeman employed on foot patrol.
Testified that he passed Ichiro Honda in the vicinity of
Fusako Aikawa's apartment early in the morning on the
night of the murder.

Two taxi drivers.
Each swore that on the night of a murder they had picked
up Ichiro Honda in the small hours and carried him to
the vicinity of Yotsuya Sanchome.

The manager of the Meikei-so.
Testified that Ichiro Honda had been his tenant.

Friends of Fusako Aikawa and Mitsuko Kosugi.
Gave evidence on the relationship of the accused with the
murdered women.

Other witnesses, also.
But, most significantly, the accused was unable to call a
single witness to testify as to his alibi.

COLLECTING THE EVIDENCE

The Lawyers

I

Hajime Shinji hastily got up from the mattress and quilts on the floor, which made up his bed, and pulled a shirt with a dirty collar over his torso. Without pausing to choose, he grabbed the nearest tie he could find and knotted it around his neck. The rest of his toilet was just as perfunctory, and within minutes he was on the way out of his room, leaving the bedding rumpled just as it was on the floor. There was a newspaper in his letterbox; without glancing at it, he rolled the pages, which still smelled of fresh ink, and stuffed it into his pocket and hurried off down the street.

Such had been the daily pattern of Hajime Shinji's life since he had graduated from the Regal Institute of Law and Research and begun work as an attorney at the Hatanaka Law Office.

On the station platform he bought two bottles of milk and gulped them down as he waited for the train. It arrived, and he was borne along in the throng and squeezed into the crowded compartment.

Shinji was not tall—a mere five feet three inches—but his swarthy face and muscular body gave him an appearance of intrepidity. His main problem nowadays was that he was beginning to lose interest in the work that had so fascinated him when he had first joined the law office. As his curiosity had become blunted, everything he did seemed to become reduced to mere routine and became meaningless to him. The courts, which had once seemed to him to be the personification of legal solemnity, now seemed no more than gray buildings where the same futile arguments were continuously repeated. Hajime Shinji was bored.

The chief of the law office where he worked was Kentaro Hatanaka. A senior figure in the profession, he had completed two terms as president of his local lawyers' association and was well known for the articles he wrote for magazines. He had saved many men from the death sentence and was much in demand as an appeal lawyer. But he had his enemies. They would say of him that he courted publicity, or that, with his reputation, he took work away from other lawyers. It was further alleged by his critics that he only took on cases when victory seemed certain. And, most of all, his colleagues criticized him for taking on cases even when it seemed certain that the defendant could never pay. This was regarded as a particularly obnoxious form of self-promotion.

Shinji had no patience for such views. The reason that he had joined Hatanaka's practice in the first place had been his deep sense of respect for this upright old man, alone in the world without wife or child, a humanist whose whole life rotated around trials in court, and who applied himself to everything he did in a manner that made it clear that he believed it to be worth doing.

And yet, despite his respect for Hatanaka, Shinji's life had recently come to seem empty. For his ambition had always been to be a judge and not a lawyer. It had been this dream that had sustained him through all those night classes at the Regal Institute after his grueling day's work as a forwarding clerk at a department store. When, to reduce the long vista of study that lay before him, he had opted for the attorney's course rather than the judicial one, he had felt guilty; he was letting society down, he thought, merely for considerations of his own welfare. And this feeling still remained with him.

A lawyer should be proud of his profession; he knew that. But what was the purpose of a life passed as a public defendant in so many trivial cases? It had become his lot to defend petty filchers, sneak thieves, and demented people who set fire to garbage piles and were accused of arson. Once, he had been involved in a case where a teenage boy had stabbed a taxi driver in order to rob him of the princely sum of two thousand yen. His ambition was to become involved in some great and dramatic case where love and hate were intertwined; gradually he had come to realize that, in real life, such cases did not exist for him.

Such, then, were his thoughts as he went to work today. But today, had he but known it, was different, for the Hatanaka Law Office had just accepted the Appeal Court case of Ichiro Honda.

It was a week later when Shinji was sent for by Hatanaka. He found his chief deeply ensconced in the comfortable leather chair behind his desk, smoking a pungent cigar.

"Sit down," the old man said. "Yes, there will do. Now, you have read the reports of the Ichiro Honda murder trial, haven't you?"

"Yes, sir," Shinji replied. "I even went to one of the sessions, as the defending counsel, Wada, was my senior at law school."

"Indeed? Well, Wada will be helping us in the appeal case, too. A serious-minded fellow, that. All right in his way, but lacks flexibility, wouldn't you agree? He's too cautious; unimaginative, too. Well, I won't ask you to comment on your senior."

The old man fell silent for a moment, his worn-out eyes fixed upon the drifting smoke of his cigar. Then he began to speak again.

"What do you think of the Honda case?"

Shinji had observed Honda in the prisoner's box at the trial, although he had mostly only seen his profile. To tell the truth, he had felt no particular interest in this man who had sat with downcast eyes as the prosecutor had launched into a peroration on how he had strangled women merely to satisfy his abnormal sexual instincts.

"Well, I got the impression that although Honda is essentially a weak man, he could, nonetheless, be capable of the cold-blooded acts of which he was accused."

He picked his words carefully and the old lawyer detected this and smiled.

"Yes, well, I daresay you are right. But nevertheless I'm not satisfied. It doesn't fit, somehow; murder doesn't go with my image of the defendant."

He paused again and then went on.

"Think of it this way. We know that Honda was a lady's man. Why, then, did he only become a monster with those three women? With so many victims of his sexual charm, why only those three? Did he try it and fail in other cases, I wonder? If he is such a pervert, did he have, shall we say, unconsummated affairs? Were there others he tried to strangle without success?"

"I don't think the police went into this aspect far enough. They were just out for a conviction; that's their job, I suppose. But I agree that the other women of his acquaintance should have been investigated. I suppose they didn't want to come forward for obvious reasons."

"Quite. So I've got a little job for you. I want you to contact Honda's other girlfriends and see what you can find out." Hatanaka looked quizzically at Shinji, blowing a smoke ring the while.

"But how can I find them?"

"Oh, that's easy enough; I've got a list. Here it is. Wada got a detective agency to track them all down. Of course, it's only a fraction of the women he has been involved with, but

103

it will do for a start. Find out if he ever seemed violent or threatening with them."

He passed the list across the desk, and Shinji studied it. Names and brief personal histories appeared, together with sketch maps of the apartments and workplaces of the women.

"Those are all that Honda remembers for sure, it seems. There were plenty more, but he says that they were all listed in his hunting diary, which he claims vanished from his hideout."

"Hunting diary?"

The old man explained.

"Did he really keep such a diary, do you think?"

"Well, if he did, and if we can find it, it could be an important key to this case. But for the time being, concentrate on the women we know about, and keep me informed."

He dropped his glance back to the documents on his desk as a symbol of dismissal.

During the next week Shinji applied himself to the task that Hatanaka had given him whenever he had a spare moment between his routine cases. Not only was this a big case by his standards: he had another reason of his own for being so interested in it. For on the list of Honda's conquests, a mere five women, there was one name that he recognized. The name and the personal history fitted. They belonged to a clerk at a lending library whom Shinji had known at school.

This coincidence struck Shinji as being ironic and in a way amusing. But was there not something of destiny in it, too?

2

Shinji decided to tackle the two most difficult women first, the ones who had refused to say anything to the police. He felt like a child saving the best things on his plate till the end. But after all he could get nothing out of either of those two. In one case, he had gone to a modern apartment block in Meguro; the door had been opened by a woman cradling a baby in her arms. She drove him away fiercely, treating him as if he were a door-to-door salesman or something. It was hardly surprising, he reflected; what married woman was going to endanger her position by talking about an old romance with a convicted murderer?

The third woman on his list was a Miss Kyoko Matsuda, aged nineteen, working in a coffee shop in Shinjuku. He decided to drop in there on the way to the office in Hibiya.

When he got there, he found that the shop was tucked under a bridge that carried the Koshu Kaido expressway over a humbler road. It was a cheap nighttime drinking area, and the neon signs and signboards looked dusty in the strong sunshine of the day. There was a big sign outside the shop: MORNING SERVICE. COFFEE AND TOAST. He went in. As he had expected, it was not crowded at this hour; the only customer was a man immersed in a racing paper.

"Is Miss Kyoko Matsuda in?"

The cashier to whom he had put this question nodded in the direction of a cheap restaurant opposite. "She's gone to early lunch over there."

"Can you tell me what kind of clothes she is wearing?"

The woman looked at him suspiciously for a moment, her surprise creasing the heavy makeup she wore even by day. Eventually she shrugged and replied, "She's in a yellow cardigan." Shinji thanked her and left the shop.

The restaurant to which he had been directed was long and low; in his fancy, it looked like a stranded eel. Arrayed in the windows of the narrow frontage were wax models of the various dishes served: peas boiled in honey and sweet bean jam, azuki bean soup with rice cake, rice balls, a few Chinese dishes, pork cutlets. He pushed his way in through the low door.

Inside, all the customers were women; there was not a male to be seen. He quickly identified Kyoko Matsuda; she was sitting at a table by the door, her back to him. He took the seat opposite her.

"I apologize for disturbing you," he said, presenting his name card.

"Quite all right," she said cheerfully, still plying her chopsticks. Shinji began to feel a glimmer of hope.

Just then a waitress came up and presented him with a menu. He would have to order something; without thinking, he pointed at a dish called *tokoroten*, a vinegared seaweed jelly flavored with horseradish. Too late he regretted ordering such an eccentric dish; moreover, it was one that women tended to eat more than men. But Kyoko looked up smiling.

"How delicious! I'll have one, too." And she pushed her empty plate toward the waitress.

When they were alone, Shinji smiled at her wryly.

"I hear you were a friend of Ichiro Honda."

"Yes. About a year ago."

"Did he come to the coffee shop, then?"

"No." She shook her head and went on. "He was sitting next to me at the cinema. That's how I met him. He told me he was a second-generation American Japanese, and my aunt lives in San Francisco, so that's how we got talking. I found him interesting, and we both got the same idea at once—to go out and paint the town red together. We went to a bar I know and drank gin fizzes—lots of them." She giggled.

"And then?" asked Shinji.

She concentrated on her food for a moment, plunging her chopsticks busily into the bowl.

"And then nothing. He said good night and I went home."

Shinji cursed the clumsiness of his interrogation. He would have to do better than this. How could he get the answer he wanted questioning her in this way?

The waitress brought over two dishes of *tokoroten*, and Kyoko attacked hers wolfishly. Shinji followed suit but got too much horseradish in his first mouthful; the pungency assailed his sinuses.

He tried again, deciding to be more blunt.

"You became lovers, of course. So tell me what you think. Was he as abnormal as the papers say?"

She shrugged her shoulders and dilated her nostrils.

"You're asking me the same thing as that policeman did

who came here the other day. Asked if he ever tried to strangle me."

"And?"

"Of course he didn't—what do you think he was, a pervert or something? I'll tell you this, though: he was really
passionate—the most passionate man I've known," she
added self-importantly.

"Did you take him home with you?"

"Who, me? You must be joking. My apartment block is
full of respectable families who like to spy on a working
girl."

"I see. How many times did you meet him altogether,
then?"

"Well, maybe ten times or so—I forget."

Shinji smiled to himself; a likely story, indeed, he thought.
Honda never used his women more than once or twice, tir-
ing of them quickly and moving on. The girl was boasting
or disguising her injured pride.

Kyoko had finished her *tokoroten*. "Pay for mine, will
you?" she said. "I've got to be off—if you want anything
else, come and see me in the coffee shop." And she got up
and left without further ceremony.

Not a word of inquiry about Honda. The affair had just
been another small incident in her life. Shinji dropped some
coins on the counter and left.

Outside, the sun was beating down more fiercely than
ever.

3

On the following day, Shinji visited the two remaining women on his list. First he went to see a chanson singer who worked at a music café on the Ginza. Before setting forth, he rang the establishment and inquired into her exact schedule for stage appearances. It was thus that he made his way down the stairs of the Salon de D at 3 P.M., passing on the way a poster upon which was emblazoned in large letters the name of the woman he had come to see. At the entrance they charged him 150 yen, giving him a ticket good for one drink and telling him that all further drinks would cost him a uniform 150 yen.

He made his way inside. It was pitch dark, only a spotlight playing upon the woman on the stage, who seemed to be whispering rather than singing into the microphone into which she leaned like a lover. Shinji took a seat at the back and watched and listened; this was the woman he had come to see.

Finally the song came to an end, the woman throwing her arms forward theatrically as if to embrace the microphone; the spotlight faded and simultaneously the house lights came on. There were, as he had expected, hardly any other customers around at this time of day. So far, so good. He summoned the white-coated waiter and asked him to present his compliments to Shoko Toda, handing over his business card as he made his request.

A few minutes passed, and then a statuesque woman in a

backless black satin dress came over to him, holding his card in her hand as if it were a talisman. She presented herself and, in most formal language, asked how she might be of service to lawyer Shinji.

The brief description in the list prepared by the detective agency described her as being about twenty-seven, but she looked much older. Shinji waved her into a chair.

"I'm defending Ichiro Honda. Could I speak to you about him, please?"

She nodded and, remarking that this was a topic to be discussed without haste or interruption, led him over to a table in a discreet position at the corner of the room. They ordered drinks and Shinji embarked upon his interrogation.

"Tell me, please, if, within the limitations of your own knowledge or experience, there was anything abnormal about Ichiro Honda?" He gazed intently into her face, trying to appear as businesslike as possible.

"I suppose what you are really asking is, did he ever try to strangle me?" the woman answered frankly. It seemed to Shinji as if Shoko Toda had been asked this question before and was prepared for it, so that she immediately grasped its import.

"It seems as if the police have already asked you the same question. Would I be correct in presuming that? Did they examine you on the same point?"

"Examined me? Forced me to speak, rather," the woman replied, her face suffused with cynicism. "They asked me again and again, 'What sort of relationship did you have with Honda?' Really! 'What sort of a relationship' . . . a pretty indelicate way of putting things, don't you think? I was furious with them; I almost wanted to spit in their faces. The relationship between a man and a woman, what passes between them in bed and so forth, really, what can it have to do with the police? Then it dawned upon me that the term 'what sort of a relationship' is just a cliché of police interrogation. But how does one answer such a question in just a few words? The relationship between a man and a woman is not such a simple thing, I told them."

The woman paused and, extracting a cigarette from her case, broke it in half carefully before putting it into a long ivory cigarette holder. She lit it, blew the smoke over Shinji's shoulder, and went on talking.

"So as a result we beat about the bush for at least an hour before I realized that what they were getting at was whether or not Ichiro Honda displayed any abnormal behavior. It became clear to me that they wanted me to say that he put a tie or a rope around my throat whilst we were making love. Those police! What a race apart they are, with their narrow little imaginations. To them, Lady Chatterly, the Marquis de Sade, they are nothing more than pornography; they don't know what pornography is, that's what I say." A sort of grandeur entered her speech, and she went on.

"I am an actress, or at least a woman who lives out her life on the stage. What could please me more than to play the role of Othello's wife, if that is what my audience wants. However, somewhat to my regret, I did not find Ichiro Honda to be a man of such unique and elevated tastes. He was just an ordinary man after all."

"You mean that there was nothing abnormal about him?"

"If you accept that sex is not of itself abnormal, then he was in all other respects normal." Again the cynicism showed through her mask.

"How did you meet him?"

"Well, these things are all a matter of timing, aren't they? I was lonely, needed someone to talk to and so forth, and I suppose the same applied to him. Anyway, his seduction was just like dancing. He led and I followed. It was all very smooth. Do you know what he gave me? A paper umbrella with a bull's-eye pattern! Rather original, don't you think? That appeals to a woman, you know. And that voice of his . . . so sweet, so soft, so low. He really did look like a man of mixed blood; it was very romantic. And he said his work was importing films for TV—that was romantic, too."

"And how many times did you see each other?"

"Oh, only the once. Yes, just once." And suddenly she burst into a sudden laughter that contorted her body.

A man came across the room and joined them, a man wearing tight trousers and with his hair loosely permed. It was the pianist.

"I hear you are Ichiro Honda's lawyer—the waiter told me. Look, I'd love to go and see him in prison—could you fix it up? I'll make it worth your while." The man's voice and gestures were effeminate and Shinji felt a deep repugnance as the man laid his hand on his shoulder. Was he trying to make a fool of him? he wondered. But the man seemed deadly serious. Ignoring him, Shinji stood up and addressed Shoko Toda.

"Thank you for telling me what you have. Could I ask you one more question? Do you believe that Ichiro Honda is a murderer and a pervert?"

She removed the cigarette holder from her lips.

"I am someone, perhaps the only person, who believes his apparently absurd protestations of innocence." She fell silent and began to muse, a dreamy look in her eyes, as if she was reviewing sweet memories.

He climbed the stairs and drew a deep breath as he made his way into the street. That was another world down there, its denizens, perhaps, people who feared the light of day. He made his way to the subway station at Nishi Ginza and boarded a train headed for Shinjuku. And in the tunnels he became overcome by an obsessive urge to get off at Yotsuya Sanchome. It was there, he remembered, that Ichiro Honda had had his hideout.

He cast his mind back to the trial, to the severe cross-examination of Honda by the public prosecutor on the question of the secret apartment. Honda, the prosecutor insisted, kept this lair with its supply of clothes, the better to commit his crimes. The prosecutor got quite carried away, his language becoming ever more elegiac and antiquated as he described the fiendish cunning of the criminal. The memory made Shinji smile. For to him Ichiro Honda's motives were crystal clear. The profession of an engineer was a serious one; what more natural than that he should wish to discard it for a disguise and wander the town in casual clothes?

As the prosecutor had spoken, all Honda could do was to mutter such phrases as "to refresh myself" in response to the barrage of questions and accusations. Honda's demeanor was that of a man who has given up trying to explain himself; this plainly left the judge with an unfavorable impression of him despite the attempts of the defense to explain that Honda's changes of clothing had been quite innocent, that all he was seeking was a sense of freedom. How could the world possibly be convinced that the freedom that Honda sought was just the freedom to seduce women? Shinji sat crushed into the corner of his seat reflecting that it was not so much the law as morality that had brought its guns to bear upon Ichiro Honda. With morality on the side of the prosecution, what chance could the defense have?

So even when the defense lawyer had spoken of the existence of Honda's diary and of how it had vanished, and also when he had spoken of the booby trap set in the wardrobe, the response of those who listened had been disbelief tinged with secret laughter.

Shinji obeyed his instinct and alighted at Yotsuya Sanchome, making his way to the pay phone in a small tobacconist. He rang the Wada law office and asked for the address of Honda's hideout. The clerk at the other end of the phone kept him waiting for some time; it was plain that the Wada law office, having lost their exclusivity over Honda, had lost some of their interest in the case.

The sun beat down on Shinji's head as he waited. At last the clerk came back and grudgingly, it seemed, gave him instructions as to how to get to the Meikei-so. It all seemed quite simple.

"Turn left by the sushi shop, you say, and then walk fifteen yards. Is that all?" Shinji scribbled feverishly on the memo pad by the phone. A ten-minute walk, that was all, it seemed. He made his way down the road. It was a very quiet area: there was a telephone exchange, a lumberyard—those were the sort of places that stood around the Meikei-so.

It was a two-story building faced with unpainted mortar, a simple enough place. A stairway ran up the side and along the outer corridor; anyone could come and go freely. *Ideal for a hideout,* Shinji thought.

On the corner door of the ground floor there was a small sign, which read "Manager." Shinji knocked on the door; it was opened by a woman who took one look at him, turned around and shouted "Darling!" before making her way back inside. She looked haggard and worn-out; a few lank hairs were glued to her forehead by sweat.

The manager proved to be a man of about forty with a pale and puffy face. It appeared that he was a jobbing tailor, for he wore a tape measure around his neck. Shinji presented his name card and asked about the apartment that Ichiro Honda had rented.

"Oh, you mean Mr. Ueda's room. It's just the way it was."

"You haven't rented it out yet?"

"Well, since all this happened, the owner wasn't sure what to do, but then we got a letter from Mr. Ueda's family saying that they would like to keep the apartment on until everything is settled. So it's left just as it was."

Shinji noticed that the manager still referred to Honda as

"Ueda," the name under which the room had been rented. He asked if he could see the room, and the manager readily assented, slipping on a pair of sandals and reaching for a bunch of keys.

"I'm stuck to my sewing machine all day long, so I welcome the chance to get away," he confided as he led Shinji up the stairway. He came to a door and opened it; the air inside was musty.

Shinji saw an iron bedstead, a wardrobe like a locker, a wooden table, and two chairs. The manager opened the window with some difficulty. "Should open them once in a while, I suppose," he murmured.

"Did Honda have many visitors?"

"No one in particular. I used to think it odd, but then he told me he was a scenario writer and only took the room to work privately, so I thought no more of it. But he was such a quiet and nice person; I wish I hadn't testified against him, you know, that he had an adhesive plaster on his face when he moved out, but I really didn't mean ... you know, I didn't understand . . ." The manager smiled weakly, his face revealing his fear that his evidence had put the rope around Honda's neck.

"There's only one other thing that I remember . . . well, it was my wife, really. She swears she heard the sound of a woman weeping in Mr. Ueda's room one day when he was out. Sounds like a ghost story, doesn't it? It made the police laugh, anyway."

"About when would that have been?"

"Let me see . . . it would have been six months before Mr. Ueda was arrested, I would say."

Shinji thanked him and left the Meikei-so.

Walking back along the street, he reflected upon what the manager had told him. Could it be true, this story of a woman weeping in Honda's room?

Judging from the fact that he still kept on referring to Honda as "Mr. Ueda" however often Shinji had corrected him, he seemed to be a man subject to *idée fixée*.

And if it was true, what could have been the meaning of those female sobs heard in the room?

Shinji thought about it for a while, but by the time he got back to the main road he had dismissed the matter from his mind. After all, he reasoned, it could not be very important, could it?

4

Getting off the suburban train, Shinji soon found a taxi outside the station.

Only one woman remained on the list that he had been given, a woman for whom he still entertained tender feelings although he had not seen her for several years. He had left her until last; soon he would see her again.

He had had to work not only through college but to get into college. He worked as a children's tutor in the evenings and on weekends; by day, he was a part-time deliveryman at a department store or a seasonal assistant at the post office. At festival and gift-giving times he had been particularly busy and heavily laden. Often he would wander the streets, his down-at-heel shoes white with dust or snow, looking for some particularly obscure address, the heavy sack on his back bulging with parcels wrapped in the distinctive paper of the store. These labors, particularly when he was working for the college entrance exam, left him little time for classes, so he tended to spend a lot of time in the college library.

Gradually he got to know the young woman who was employed there as a lending clerk; they were attracted to each other, it was plain, but much as he had wanted to date her, he rarely had the money to do it. So in all those months and years he had only met her outside the college seven, eight, perhaps ten times. And amongst those few times, he had only made love to her once, quickly and furtively in the six-by-nine-foot room where he lodged.

Eventually he passed into the college and became even more busy attending classes as well as earning his keep on the side, so they drifted apart and, in time, ceased to see each other.

This short acquaintanceship remained ingrained in his brain, banal as it now sometimes seemed to him, this brief affair between a struggling student and a library clerk. But how often he wondered as he sat in the taxi, which was climbing the slope to the college campus, do such brief, doomed lovers ever meet again? A faint expectation stirred in his breast.

The taxi came to the gates of the college, beyond which

no cars were allowed. He paid his fare and got out and began to walk toward the old brick building; the road was lined with cherry trees. The first green grass of summer was beginning to thrive on the lawn in front of the campus.

He cast his mind back to how it had been in his student days. Summer ... so hot; the lawn in front of the library would grow so fast that even weekly mowings could not keep it down. Memories ... a row of tall sunflowers; sweat that poured down him no matter how he had wiped his brow; the library, empty in the long summer vacation; a girl who worked there and always wore white blouses ... Steeped in these memories of student life, he paused for a while in front of the library before suddenly going in as if he was only doing so on second thoughts.

Inside, it was still just the same: musty and cool.

He went up to the counter. Michiko Ono, the lending clerk, was writing on a heap of small cards. Just as he remembered, she sat with a slightly bent back, her head tilted slightly at an angle that he found charming. But the former childish expression on her face was no more. He read the passing of time in the lines and wrinkles about her eyes. What those lines meant was the slow death of a human soul.

"Miss Ono," he said quietly, his voice choking a little.

She stopped her writing and looked up as if she was disgruntled at being interrupted in her task. Then recognition crept over her features, mixed with a look of mild shock. She blinked two or three times and then, in a voice throbbing with emotion, said, "Mr. Shinji! It's you! It's been a long time!"

"I was passing by so I thought I'd drop in."

"I'll be off in half an hour—we close at five-thirty."

He glanced at his wristwatch. "Well, then, maybe I can do a little research while I'm waiting. Graduates are allowed to borrow books, aren't they?"

"Yes, provided you don't take them away. Use the reading room."

"Well, do you have anything on blood types?"

She ran through her cards with a practiced hand and soon produced two volumes.

"This is all we seem to have—unless, of course, you look in the encyclopedias, too."

Thanking her, Shinji carried the books to the reading room. He had wanted to talk to her for a little longer, but he knew the library rules—no talking or disturbing other people. The books she had given him were, as one might expect in a legal library, works on forensic medicine. He extracted all he could find that he thought might be of use, noting it in a small notebook that he carried, and then closed the books and lay back in the chair, smoking aimlessly and gazing up at the dirty ceiling until Michiko came.

She had changed and was ready to go home. "Were the books useful?" she asked.

"Oh yes, thank you. I found all I wanted."

"So you are working on a case involving blood types? It must be pretty complicated."

"Yes," said Shinji, and then, summoning up his courage, "in fact, I am working on the defense of Ichiro Honda. You know, the Sobra case."

Her countenance immediately darkened. "Oh, so you have only come to see me to talk business. Am I right?"

"Frankly speaking, yes, though it's wonderful to see you again. Honda gave us the names of five women whom he could remember and . . . your name was one of them. A big coincidence, I felt," he stated sadly.

The reading room was empty apart from the two of them; it was shrouded in silence, now that he had stopped speaking, broken only by the faint cries of students indulging in sports somewhere in the distance.

In this silence, there came back to him a memory of his primary school days. School had been over, and nearly everyone had gone home. Then, too, in the distance he had heard sounds—a faltering étude being played in a distant classroom.

And that was the time he had hit his friend who had passed an insulting remark about his father. Shinji's father had been a mine broker and thus rarely at home, so the other children used to tease him by saying that his father must be in prison. Even when he grew up, Shinji believed he knew how children with fathers in prison must feel.

Bringing himself back to the present, he continued.

"Yes, a coincidence, one I didn't really want to believe. So I put off seeing you till the last."

Michiko hesitated a moment before speaking. Then, "It's true," she said quietly. "I did know him. I needed someone to talk to, someone who would speak to me in an endearing way. And he did that, which is why I went with him to the hotel. It was only once, though. You might as well know that." She gathered up the books and walked toward the door and then, turning, spoke again.

"You must think I'm gullible. And worse still, I got pregnant by him."

Shinji felt as if the ground was opening under his feet.

"Michiko! You can't have!"

She smiled back at him quietly. "But I did. And my son is now nine months old. He has begun to speak baby talk."

Shinji was flabbergasted. Michiko had borne Honda's child. There had been nothing in the detective's report about that. He ran after her. She stopped and gazed out over the campus, not looking at him.

"Yes, you must be surprised. My mother takes care of him, you know, so I can continue to work."

"But didn't you want Honda to recognize the child as his?"

"Why? It's nothing to do with him. I decided to have the child on my own responsibility," she said firmly. "So it's mine, not his."

Shinji realized that this woman had voyaged to lands of experience that were far beyond his ken.

"And you feel no anger or hatred toward him for his irresponsibility?"

"How can he be irresponsible if he doesn't even know about it?"

Shinji was stumped for a reply. Eventually, he spoke.

"If it had been me . . . if I had fathered your child, would you have still kept silent?"

His words seemed to turn to bubbles as they fell from his mouth, so that his question was almost inaudible. It sounded as if he was speaking from the bottom of a deep lake.

"Had it been you, of course I would have visited you and asked you if you would have liked to be the father."

She smiled at him and turned and walked out of the library, Shinji following her. They reached the gate. Shinji knew that he had nothing more to ask her. To ask if Ichiro Honda had put a rope around her neck was plainly quite meaningless.

Michiko turned. "Good-bye," she said, and was gone.

Watching her retreating back, Shinji was at a loss as to what to do.

Of one thing he was certain beyond all doubt. He had lost something and it was gone forever.

5

Shinji climbed the cavelike staircase, his footsteps the only sound echoing in the dim gloom. Up and up: seven floors, and his feet, worn out by walking all day, felt like lead. After six the elevators ceased to function and the hall lights were turned off. At last he reached the seventh floor and paused to wipe the sweat from his brow.

He opened the office door. Here, too, dusk had fallen deeply. Mutsuko Fujitsubo, secretary to his chief, was sitting all alone, a vacant expression on her face. She was a modest-looking but ill-favored girl, with her heavy glasses with their thick, amber-colored rims, and she had joined the office immediately after graduating from junior college two years before.

"Hello! Sorry to be back so late! Is the old man still around?"

"Yes. He's reading the report from the detective agency." She pointed resignedly to the door at the far end of the office, worn-out by the long wait.

Shinji washed his face with cold water and, refreshed, went into Hatanaka's room, the girl following him, her shorthand pad in her hand.

The old man straightened up in his deep chair. "You've been working hard, I see." He spoke gruffly, his voice seeming strangled by phlegm. Shinji sat down and without further ado took out his notebook and, watching the girl out of the corner of his eye to see that she did not fall behind, began to make his report. In all that silent building about which the dusk had fallen, it seemed as if only his voice could be heard.

"Today, I completed my interviews with all the women on the list. It transpired that they had all been interviewed by the police, and that the thrust of their questions was the same as mine: did Ichiro Honda ever attempt to strangle them?"

"And did he?"

"I couldn't get a word out of two of them. And even with the others, you must realize, it wasn't an easy question to come right out with. But the three who would talk . . . two denied it plainly, and it was clear to me that there was no such incident in the third case."

"No wonder they were not called to give evidence by the prosecutors," snapped the old man.

"Yes, but why didn't the defense summon them?" asked Shinji.

"Because the fools were trying to cover up his relationships with women! They thought it best to conceal the fact that he was a lady killer; I disagree with them entirely, of course. Honda Ichiro was on trial in a court of law, not a court of morals!"

Just what I thought, too, thought Shinji approvingly. He went on: "I did find out something quite interesting today, though. Michiko Ono, who works at a library, has a nine-month-old son and claims that the father is Ichiro Honda. If we work on her, she might be persuaded to give evidence on our behalf."

"And for how long did her relationship with Honda last?"

"Only just the once," said Shinji sheepishly, and the old man groaned audibly.

"But the child isn't mentioned in the detective agency report. I wonder why she told you about it?"

Shinji realized that he would have to confess. "Well, I knew her when I was a student," he said. "I was in love with her for a time. I suppose that's why she told me."

The old man was silent. The secretary, her pencil stilled, set her shoulders in a pose suggesting astonishment. The sun had finally set, and the desk light was hardly enough to see by. "I'll put on the light," said Shinji, breaking the silence.

He got up and went to the switch, his motions disturbing the air of the room, which had become like a sealed tomb. The old man slowly lit a fresh cigar.

"And does this young woman, what's her name?"—gazing at the report—"Michiko Ono, does she have any intention of telling Honda about the happy event?"

"She says it's nothing to do with Ichiro Honda, that it is her affair entirely," replied Shinji.

"Perhaps because the child's father might be a murderer?"

"She doesn't believe he committed any of the crimes."

"Why do all these women believe in his innocence, I wonder?" mused the old man. "Is he particularly good to women, do you think?"

"That's the main point about him," said Shinji. "His abnormality, if we are looking for one, seems to lie in the fact that he can get inside women and win their sympathy. He deceived them all, but none of those women see it that way. I just don't know how to explain it, but plainly it's true." He was surprised that his growing familiarity with the case had planted inside him feelings about Ichiro Honda of which he had not been aware. This did not mean that for a moment he approved of Honda's behavior.

The old man seemed to be satisfied with Shinji's report. He jotted a few notes down on a pad, but Shinji could not see what they were. Finally he looked up and said, "I went to see him today, you know." There seemed to be almost a tone of intimacy in the way he said "him." "He's been in jail for three months now, and it seems to have turned him into a mere shadow of himself. It's impossible to visualize him as

an attractive man who can sweep women off their feet. The
death sentence has plainly knocked him all of a heap. I tried
to put some life back into him; I advised him to reconstruct
his lady-killer's diary instead of just moping in his cell. He
can do it if he tries; being a computer engineer, he has a better memory than most people. He should be able to remember most of it, given time—I'd bet on it." He took out a
fresh cigar and bit off the end.

"What do you think is the salient point of this case—the
one we're going to have to overcome at the appeal?" he
asked as he fiddled with his lighter.

"The defendant's rare blood type."

"I agree. They found blood under their fingernails—
minute quantities, but enough. It's one of the first things
you look for in cases of strangulation; often the victim man-
ages to scratch the killer's face. Well, when they first analyzed, they were a bit cursory and put it down as AB. But
after Honda's arrest they found that he had a rare group—
AB Rh-negative. So they went back and analyzed again and
found that the blood was not merely AB but also Rh-negative. So their suspicions were confirmed—proved to all ex-
tents and purposes. This evidence as good as put the rope
around his neck."

"Yes," said Shinji, "and there's a related bit of evidence—
the sperm type. They detected type AB in the vaginas of the
victims. Only this evidence is less overwhelming; you can
identify a blood type from either saliva or sperm, but you
can't go further than A, B, AB, or O in such cases—it's only
from blood that you can detect Rh-negative." Shinji

thought that his earlier research in the library had been useful after all.

"Very good. Now, blood types apart, there is one other bit of evidence that weighs heavily against the defendant, in my view."

"The lack of an alibi," replied Shinji, as promptly as if he were a primary school student who had done his homework well. He was enjoying this dialectic with his senior.

"Indeed, yes. On the fifth of November, whilst the first murder was being committed, Ichiro Honda claims to have been with Fusako Aikawa. However, on the nineteenth of December, on the night that Fusako Aikawa was killed, he claims to have been with Mitsuko Kosugi, who was inconveniently killed next. This non-alibi that he submits in place of an alibi interests me greatly. On first study, it looks like a cock-and-bull story, doesn't it? If we are to believe him, he would have perfect alibis—except that, unfortunately, the women who could give them to him were murdered in their turn. Absurd, you say? But it raises interesting possibilities, too. Let's just stop and think about motive, shall we? Contrast Honda's rather unconvincing excuses for alibis with the question of motive. What motive did the prosecution put forward, do you remember?"

"Yes, sir. They claim that he strangled the women during sexual intercourse to satisfy his abnormal sexual tastes. And in support of this they got the family doctor who attends upon him and his wife to testify as to his impotence when he is with his wife."

"Correct. The court was convinced of the view that he was

a sexual criminal. However, I don't agree. If his motive was sexual perversity, then why stop at two or at most three? It's inconsistent, isn't it? Why spare all the other women? He should have felt the same abnormal feelings toward them— and we know that he didn't. So let me present a hypothesis. Let us imagine that the killer of all three women is called 'X.'

"Now, if X equals Honda, then you can be excused for thinking that all three murders were committed for sexual reasons.

"But if X isn't Honda, if it's someone quite different, then we are left with another motive, one we didn't think about when we thought that X was Honda. Do you follow me?"

Shinji thought for a while. "I see," he said at last. "You mean that X was trying to entrap Honda?"

"Precisely, a trap. And I will tell you this. X, having committed the murders, didn't seek to put the blame on Honda to save his own skin. How perfectly it was all contrived! No, something far more deliberate was involved.

"The women were murdered in order to frame Ichiro Honda."

He spelled out these last words slowly and with great clarity. After a pause to let his words sink in, he continued. "Thus, in my opinion, the motive of X was a grudge against Honda. I felt increasingly sure of this when I was talking to the defendant today. What I now need is a list of all people who might hold such a grudge against him—that's why I want him to reconstruct his diary."

The old man spoke with increasing ardor, carrying Shinji

129

along with him. It was like listening to some great advocate making a speech in court. The logic was beautiful, but could it hold together? Shinji doubted it; there was too much of a jump somewhere.

"I think," went on Hatanaka, "that the rock-firm, the adamantine evidence presented to the court has been deliberately contrived by someone. It is the cunning work of a human being, not a sequence of accidents."

"But can you convince the court of that?"

"Probably not. I must find evidence no less hard with which to confront the evidence against us."

Shinji did not ask him how he intended to do this. He was overwhelmed by the old man's sense of commitment.

"So," the senior lawyer went on, "I'm going to make full use of that detective agency. Luckily the father-in-law is paying the bills, and he is rich—we can spend as much as we like. Acting on my conviction that all the evidence is planted, I'm going to start off by finding out how one gets hold of Rh-negative blood if one wants to." He relit his cigar, which had gone out. "My mind is full of the righteous justice of the ancient Greeks," he went on. "To them, Justice was the median line drawn between the defendant and his accusers. In this case, someone has tampered with that line, and I'm going to put it back where it belongs."

The conversation was over, and Hatanaka stood up to leave. Shinji helped the secretary close the windows. Outside, the robe of night had fallen on the city; gazing into the dark streets, he felt that, against all the evidence, the zeal and devotion of one old man could possibly change the whole balance of the trial after all. The vast, dark sky was no broader than the old man's commitment.

Behind him, Hatanaka shuffled out of the door, stooping, his briefcase in his hand.

The Blood Bank

I

A week passed before the old man sent for Shinji again.

"I've got another job for you," he said. "Sit down and take a look at this." He passed over three typewritten pages stapled together. "It's the report I got back from the detective agency today. You will see that it lists the names, addresses, and workplaces of six people, together with an outline of their daily schedules."

Shinji looked at the papers. "Yes, I've got it," he finally announced. "But what do you want me to do?"

"Well, the blood type of everyone on that list is AB Rh-negative."

"The same type as Ichiro Honda, in fact?"

"Correct. And what percentage of the population has that type, do you think?"

Shinji cast his mind back to his studies in the library. The book had said that fifteen percent of Caucasians had Rh-negative blood, but that in the case of Orientals, the ratio fell to only half a percent.

132

"One in two hundred, I seem to remember."

The old man smiled. "No, much less. Certainly one in two hundred exhibit the rhesus factor, but AB Rh-negative narrows it down even further. Only ten percent of Japanese have AB blood. So the answer to my question is one in two thousand!"

"So how many does that make for the whole of Tokyo?"

"Well, taking the population of Tokyo at ten million, that makes five thousand."

"From amongst whom you have listed six?"

"Ah, but five thousand is a sort of meaningless statistic. How many of those five thousand know that their blood is AB Rh-negative? In wartime, people tend to know their blood type, but not in peace. To be honest, I don't even know my type." He laughed mischievously, rolling the cigar around in his mouth.

Shinji, on the other hand, knew that his blood was type AB. At primary school he had always worn a tag with his blood type on it. This was one of his small remaining memories of the war. But he had never had cause to check it since. And, come to think of it, Rhesus types were discovered during the war, when transfusions became common. Nowadays, if people have Rhesus-factor blood, it is a matter of importance to them, but in his schooldays it had been unknown. Perhaps he, too, was Rh-negative.

If that was so, and if he had no alibi for the times of the murders, then he, too, could be a suspect.

"Yes. Even amongst people who know where they fall in

the A, B, and O system, there are very few who know if they are Rhesus or not," said the old man.

"So how do people find out?"

"There are two ways."

"Well, I suppose if you have a blood transfusion, you know."

"Yes. And what's the other way?"

Shinji was stumped. The old man laughed triumphantly and explained.

"People who give their blood for transfusion, of course!"

"You mean donors? And people who sell their blood?"

"Yes. And I'm not interested in fresh transfusions, only in blood that is stored."

"You mean in blood banks?"

"Yes. And, you know, you don't deposit your blood and draw it back when you need it in a blood bank. Most, if not all, blood-bank blood is sold. And the banks keep details of the people who sell to them."

"Ah! So you mean that you can get lists of AB Rh-negative people from a blood bank?"

"Yes, and that is what I have had done—hence the list in your hand. Inquiries were made at every blood bank in Tokyo. There were twenty-seven Rh-negative people on their books, of whom six were also AB. Statistically rather high, but there you are."

The old man's plan began faintly to dawn on Shinji. It seemed a long shot at best, a dangerous gamble at worst.

"I know it sounds funny, but when we discuss it in this way my imagination forces me to behave as if I were the criminal," the old man continued. "What I mean is that I try and imagine I am the criminal, get inside his mind. If I wanted to frame Ichiro Honda by leaving his blood group at the scene of the crime, how would I set about it? Well, of course, I'd go to a blood bank to find people with the type I was after. So what do you think I did next? I caused inquiries to be made at all the blood banks to see if anyone had during the last year made inquiries about Rh-negative donors. And, you know, there was one." He sounded almost triumphant.

He took another document out of the folder in front of him. Shinji reflected on the careful attention to detail that had made Hatanaka such a good criminal lawyer. The old man lit a cigar and went on.

"In the beginning of last September, I learned, there was an inquiry about AB Rh-negative blood made to several banks. The cause given was that it was needed for a newborn baby. Babies born to mothers with Rh-negative blood have to have all their blood changed to Rh-negative, or they die. The condition is called 'Hemolytic disease of the newborn.'

"Well, I next asked for which hospital the request was made. It was a hospital in Toshima ward. So I rang them, and, would you believe it, they have not had a single such case in the last twelve months!"

"So the call was a fake."

"Absolutely correct."

The old man had finally picked up the traces of the person who had entrapped Ichiro Honda. Now all he had to do was to follow the trail. Shinji stiffened with excitement.

"What was the person who made the inquiry like?" he asked.

"It was always a telephone call. But they say that the voice sounded forced."

"A man?"

"Most probably, judging from what was said. However, we must not overlook the possibility of a woman disguising her voice to sound like a man. I think we should keep an open mind."

"Well, at least they left us with our first clue. So this list comprises the names that the inquirer was given?"

"Yes. But you will observe that one of them is a woman aged forty-two. A day laborer from the flophouses. I gather that nowadays you can tell gender from blood, so let's strike her out. So just check out these five; I have a hunch that you will find that one of them sold his blood to our mysterious stranger."

So far, the old man's reasoning seemed to hold together, Shinji thought. But if his theory was true, and there existed a person who had trapped Honda, how on earth had they known his blood type?

"It seems to me," he said, "that as Ichiro Honda knew that he was AB Rh-negative since he was at college, then only his close friends and relatives would know."

"No. Anyone could have found out." The old man produced a faded newspaper clipping from his file with the air of a child removing his secret playthings from a box. "This dates back ten years. I got it from the archives of a newspaper company. It relates how a hemolytically diseased baby was saved by a transfusion in a Fukuoka hospital. And of course you can guess who the donor was. Ichiro Honda." The old man gazed at him in triumph.

"You see, it was one of the very first Rh-negative transfusions in Japan, and it was big news at the time. So it made the front page—complete with a photo of Honda." He passed the clipping over, and Shinji looked at a photo of a much younger Honda. He cast his eye over the headlines and caption.

"A.M.U. Biology Lab saves baby," he read. "All students' blood classified in American manner. A triumph for science. Student flies to Fukuoka in military plane and gives blood."

The old man chewed his cigar. "There's something else which is interesting in there," he observed. "In those days, the term 'hemolytic disease of the newborn' was not used, so they referred to it by the old medical name—'Rhesus incompatibility.' And the person who made the phone call used that expression and not the term now used. That's one reason why the phone calls were remembered at the hospitals. And the phrase in the article is 'Rhesus incompatibility.' So it's pretty obvious, isn't it?"

"You mean that you think that the mystery caller had read the article?"

"That's exactly what I think. I have no doubt that the caller was not involved with any baby at all. I feel certain that he or she was the elusive X. So you go and track down those five men, and meanwhile I think I'll go to the prison and encourage Honda in his reconstruction of his diary."

Could the old man be right? As he said, only checking with the five men would tell. He stood up to go, but the old man stopped him.

"I learn from the university that Ichiro Honda was a model student in every way. Always top of his class and an upstanding moral type."

"So what came over him to change?" asked Shinji, but the old man gave him no reply.

Had Honda been a hypocrite at the university? Shinji wondered. Or had he become as he was as a reaction to his student life at Asia Moral University?

Why do some men become womanizers? Shinji would have dearly liked to know, but at present his main task was to hunt down the person who had framed Ichiro Honda.

He picked up the papers and left the room.

Shinji left the office just before noon; the bright daylight, after the gloomy office, dazzled his eyes. Who should he visit first? he wondered. At all costs, he must get his report back to the old man as quickly as possible. He had been through the list carefully several times but still could not make up his mind. He cast his mind back over the names and details on the detective's report. They were:

1. *Yuzo Osawa, aged 58, day laborer. Present address: Fukumae Ryokan, Asahicho, Shinjuku. Family and former address unknown.*
Goes to Shinjuku Ward Employment Exchange every day and is engaged in road construction, mostly job-creation schemes financed by the Ward.

(Note.) Dines at a cheap restaurant called "Renko," near his lodging, every evening. Always has the same meal: two cups of cheap white spirit and a bowl of mince and curdled beans, his favorite dish. Drinks to get tipsy, but not drunk.

Best times to approach him are either outside the Employment Exchange or else during his evening meal.

Well, thought Shinji, *most people would consider him to be a failure in life, but who is to say that he is not living as he wants to and enjoying it?*

2. Seiji Tanikawa, aged 23, works for T Film Processing Laboratory Co., Ltd. High school graduate. Present address: 12 X-chome, Shimorenjaku, Mitaka City. This is his company's dormitory for single men.

(Note.) Generally satisfactory attitude to work. Works late two or three nights a week. Does not frequent coffee bars or restaurants, etc., but on Mondays and Fridays, when he rarely works late, he visits a Turkish bath in Kanda. The girl he always employs is called Yasue Terada. For further details, contact this researcher.

Tanikawa's salary is 28,000 yen a month including all overtime payments. He sends 5,000 yen a month to his mother in Fukushima. Our research indicates that his charges and tips at the Turkish bath come to not less than 2,000 yen a time. This implies that when he goes twice in a week as is his custom, this would con-

sume nearly 20,000 yen a month. Adding on the money he sends his mother, the dormitory charges, money he spends on presents of sushi to the girl in the bathhouse, and the minimum required to keep body and soul alive, his monthly expenditure cannot be below 30,000 yen. We believe he has a side income through making and selling some kind of films.

A man who is gradually getting mired in the mud and will probably sink into it in due course, thought Shinji.

3. Rosuke Sada, aged 33, a salesman with H Cosmetics Co., Ltd., Suginami branch office. Present address: Tachibana-so, 2-chome, Asagaya, Suginami-ku.

A university graduate. Married with no children.

(Note.) His sales area is Setagaya, Suginami, Shibuya, and Nakano wards. His customers are mostly drawn from the upper class. His performance is in the upper-middle range; however, we have reason to believe that he has recently been supplementing his income by selling jewelry supplied to him by a college friend. Monthly income over 40,000 yen. His routine is hard to predict, owing to the nature of his calling, but he regularly lunches at a German-style restaurant called "Hamburg" in Shinjuku. After work he either goes home and watches television, or else goes out to a neighboring coffee shop and talks to the women who run it. Seems to be interested in women.

140

This man, thought Shinji, *is my highest common multiple.*

4. *Nobuya Mikami, aged 18, a live-in bartender at the Bar B in Hanazono-cho, Shinjuku. Present address: as shown above.*

(Note.) Bar B is a gay bar. Its special characteristic is that all the employees are young men under the age of 19, and none of them wear drag. There are very few casual customers; most of the clientele resort there for purposes of sodomy. Many established customers do not even bother to turn up, particularly persons of a certain social status. Instead, they phone in to place their requirements. The owner, who calls himself "Mama," arranges liaisons suitably in such circumstances. Minimum charge is 3,000 yen, but it tends to be very much higher according to the client's wallet and tastes. Some of the young men who work there have been given houses by their patrons; those who relate closely to foreigners often go on overseas trips.

Interesting, thought Shinji.

5. *Kotaro Yamazaki, aged 26, an intern at the Y University Hospital. Present address: c/o Muneda, Tsuji-cho, Otsuka, Bunkyo-ku.*

(Note.) He has boarded at the above address since he was a student. His routine out of hours is irregular—sometimes he studies for his medical exams, at other times he goes out to see foreign movies or baseball games, or else to drink.

However, he regularly frequents a local coffee shop called "Blue-bird." He is almost invariably there at lunchtime, for it is immediately next to his hospital.

Well, thought Shinji, *this man must know quite a lot about blood types and the collection of blood.*

So Shinji decided to tackle the medical intern first. He thought that at least he would have a chance of catching him at his favorite coffee shop during the lunch hour. Looking at his watch, he saw that it was already 11:30.

He set off for Ochanomizu, where the hospital was situated, but en route he had an idea. He got off the train and phoned a journalist friend of his whose office was not far away. He felt that he would be better off with a journalist's business card, so he rang his friend and asked him for the favor of two or three of his cards, explaining that he was involved in interviewing people and would find them useful. "Of course," his friend said, and he made his way to the newspaper office. Resisting his friend's invitation to take lunch together, he then continued on his way.

He got to the university and called Kotaro Yamazaki on the internal phone. The voice that answered him was heavy and unpromising.

"I am from the *Daily News,*" he announced. "I am writing an article on the devotion of blood donors and wonder if you could spare me a few minutes of your time."

"You've come to the wrong person." The voice was cold and aloof.

"But the G Blood Bank told me that you were a voluntary donor of Rh-negative blood . . ."

"That's very peculiar. I haven't given blood for years."

"Nevertheless, couldn't you spare me a little time? It won't take long, I assure you." Shinji adopted his most persuasive tones.

"Really, this is an imposition," replied the voice angrily, but finally, with a great show of reluctance, he consented to meet Shinji at the Bluebird coffee shop. He turned up there twenty minutes later and proved to be a tall and handsome man. He identified Shinji by the fact that he was the only person there sitting alone and sat down opposite him.

"I'm Yamazaki. What can I do for you?"

"I would like to ask you a few questions, as I understand that you have been the donor of a rare type of blood. Can I begin by asking if your involvement is in any way due to the fact that you yourself are a doctor?"

Yamazaki stared at the reporter's name card, which Shinji had given him, turning one corner down before replacing it on the table.

"Well, as I told you on the phone, I haven't given blood for years."

"And back then? Did you donate often?"

"No. Only two or three times in all."

"And you haven't given blood recently?"

"Not for at least a year. And even then it wasn't voluntary. I received a specific request from the blood bank because of my unusual blood group. They were out of stock, it seems, and there was some emergency—a newborn baby, I believe."

"Other than that?"

"Never."

"What about between October last year and January this year?"

At this question, Yamazaki gazed at Shinji sharply, but the latter maintained his bland countenance and Yamazaki relaxed. He replied sulkily, "If I say never, I mean never! Why are you so inquisitive, might I ask?"

Shinji felt that there was nothing more to be gained from the conversation and stood up to leave. Yamazaki leaned back in his chair and, gazing up at Shinji, drawled, "Blood is a boring subject, don't you think? Now sperm, that's quite a different matter. The other day I gave an interview to a journalist from some third-rate rag or other on the topic of sperm donation. That's much more interesting, wouldn't you agree? But of course we donors are not allowed to talk about it—ethics of the trade, you might say."

He was now bantering, and so Shinji totally overlooked the significance of what he was saying and paid up and left the shop.

He went back to his office, where he found Mutsuko Fujitsubo filing papers. The old man was at the prison talking to Ichiro Honda.

"How's the reconstruction of the diary going, I wonder?" he asked, meanwhile glancing at a sheet of information from the detective agency that Mutsuko was about to file. It revealed that amongst Honda's victims there had been an elementary school teacher. The secret stains of humanity could be found in every life.

"Not too well, I'm afraid," Mutsuko replied. "It seems that Honda can't recollect as much as the old man had hoped he could. And the detective agency isn't making much progress, either. They've got literally dozens of people out on the case, but without much effect."

Shinji reflected that finding someone with a motive by reconstructing the lady killer's diary would not be as easy a task as the old man had hoped, and he sensed that Mutsuko felt the same way. If this was true, the old man would have to go to the appeal court with nothing new to present. The day for the hearing was drawing close, and Shinji felt that he had no time to lose. The murderer had left a faint footprint at the blood banks; it was up to him to go out and collect the most precise details that he could and give them to the old man.

3

Evening came, and the sun went down. On the pavement outside the cheap pub called "Renko," someone had sprinkled water in a vain attempt to lay the dust.

Shinji pushed his way through the mean rope curtain that separated the dive from the outside world. He quickly identified Yuzo Osawa as being the old man sitting by himself at the U-shaped counter and drinking *shochu*, a cheap and potent white spirit. As the researcher had suggested, there was a plate of mincemeat and bean curd in front of him. The pub was almost full, and nearly everyone was engrossed in the television screen, but when Shinji sat down beside Osawa he discovered that the screen was half hidden by a pillar from that seat. He ordered a bottle of beer.

Osawa sat next to him, cradling his glass of *shochu* in his hands as if trying to warm it. Occasionally, he would raise the glass to his lips and take a slow and careful sip. His fingernails were engrimed with oil and dust.

"Hey, old fellow! Haven't we met somewhere before!" said Shinji with forced joviality.

Osawa turned and gazed at him blankly. He cupped his ear and said, "What?" His several-day growth of stubble, peppered with white, contributed further to his generally slovenly appearance.

"I said we've met before, haven't we?"

"Oh yeah?" replied the old vagrant in negative tones, and he returned his attention to his *shochu*. He was withdrawing into his shell, and Shinji had to move quickly.

"I remember where it was. We were both in line at the same blood bank . . . let me see, the Komatsu Laboratory on the Keio line, wasn't it? I've just sold 200 cc today, so let me buy you a drink, gaffer."

"Really? Very kind, I'm sure." His voice softened perceptibly. He gulped down the remainder of his glass in one mouthful, as if afraid that this stranger might change his mind. But still the way in which he wiped his mouth with his hand betrayed how precious the liquor was to him.

With the new glass in front of him, he relaxed. "It's

O.K. for you young guys, I expect," he opened defensively. "They'll still buy your blood, I expect. But an old man like me ... they don't want us any more. Say it isn't thick enough or something."

"So you aren't selling any more? When did you last sell, then?"

"Over a year ago. The person in charge was shifted, and the new one doesn't take me seriously."

"But would you still sell if you could? I mean, if someone, anyone, came to buy, would you sell?"

"Sure I would. I'm quite healthy and besides, my blood is a rare type. Valuable, it is. Not the blood most people have, you know. I'm AB Rh-negative—only one in two thousand, you know. But still nobody comes to buy it."

The old man's speech was beginning to slur. Shinji ordered him another drink and stood up to go.

"Buy you another one sometime, old fellow," he said. The old man, his mouth full of *shochu*, almost choked as he said good-bye. Shinji left and headed toward Shinjuku Station. Well, he thought, the old laborer was no longer able to sell his blood. Who would want it, thin and alcohol-soaked as it was? Anyone seeking blood would try to get it from a younger man, someone around Ichiro Honda's age. He deleted from his mind the day laborer and the medical student. And, he reflected, X was unlikely to have approached the intern because of his medical knowledge.

At Shinjuku Station he took the Chuo line and headed for Kanda. Once the train started, he thrust his head out of the window, letting the rushing air drive the beer fumes out of his head. But as the train gathered speed, he found that the buffeting slipstream deadened his thinking. The palace moat, glittering in the summer night, flashed before his eyes; he just took in the lovers and others in gaily lit boats bobbing on the waters. Even after the sight was long gone, the white shirt and matching blouse of one such couple lingered in his eyes.

The Turkish bathhouse, Alibaba, lay about five minutes' walk from Kanda Station. Indeed, Shinji could see its garish, red neon sign from the train as it drew into the platform. However, getting to it was much more difficult than he had anticipated. He had to walk down a narrow alleyway crowded with cabarets, cheap bars, and low-class eating houses. Passing one such establishment, which specialized in skewered chicken, he had to wade through the heavy white smoke that flowed down from its extractor grill. He felt trapped. And rather than the smell of oil, he began to sense the scent of sexual desire and immorality. There was also a row of small textile wholesalers, all of whom had closed and pulled down their shutters long since, leaving the approach to the Turkish bath in pitch darkness. Alibaba stood immediately next to a public bathhouse; what a contrast, Shinji thought, between the physical cleanliness of the one and the moral pollution of the other. For, although he had never been inside such an establishment, he was well aware that they were no more than the thinnest of veils for prostitution.

The entrance was flanked by potted palms and rubber plants. Passing them, he came into the tiled outer hall, which was hidden from the inside by a wall covered in maroon and gold satin damask.

Within, the lights were low and faintly red. The red carpet had such a deep pile that it absorbed his footsteps, giving him a sense of secrecy. There was a table with a couch and several soft armchairs to one side of the lobby, where sat several men who had nominated girls and were waiting for them to be free. They were mostly reading magazines or watching TV listlessly; although there were several open bottles of beer on the table, nobody seemed to be drinking much.

He sat down, and a male attendant immediately approached him.

"Do you have anyone in particular you want to see?"

"Yes. Miss Yasue." This was the girl who, according to the detective's report, was favored by Seiji Tanikawa. "Miss Yasue, if I remember aright. You do have such a girl here?"

"Certainly, sir. Please wait for a few minutes," said the attendant with fawning politeness. "May I get you a drink in the meantime—compliments of the house, of course."

Shinji ordered a whiskey, and the attendant withdrew.

According to the detective's report, Seiji Tanikawa frequented this establishment on Mondays and Fridays—the days when he had no night work. Normally, it appeared, he came here between seven and nine—the slack period.

He noticed that the lobby was permeated by a strange, heavy odor. It was, he decided, the smell of men who were about to unload their sexual desire.

Time crawled by. Occasionally a customer sitting by the

table would get up and disappear within in answer to the attendant's summons. But they were always replaced by new arrivals from outside, some of them drunk. Sometimes a woman in sandals, wearing a red-and-white-striped wrapper over her Turkish bath girl's uniform of a red-striped brassiere and scanty pants, would emerge and see her customer off with a gay voice. Had Seiji Tanikawa gone home already, or was he still within?

As this thought crossed Shinji's mind, the curtain parted and out stepped Tanikawa. Shinji recognized him, down to the lean body, from photographs provided by the detectives. His skinny figure was emphasized by the black polo-necked sweater that he was wearing tonight. He was followed closely by a diminutive girl—obviously Yasue Terada. Tanikawa walked straight past Shinji, displaying his sunken cheeks and haggard profile.

Yasue saw him off at the entrance, tapping his bony shoulder with familiarity. Tanikawa merely shrugged his shoulders and left without a word. *For a man to visit this place twice a week* . . . , Shinji, whose private life was as clean as a sheet of blank paper, thought. He watched Tanikawa's retreating figure until it vanished from his view, convinced that in it he could sense a shadow of weakness; this man's feet were sinking into the swamp of vice.

Yasue made her way back in, but was stopped by the attendant, who whispered something to her. She came over to Shinji, but when she saw his face she was taken aback.

"You are Mr. . . ." she started, but could not finish the sentence.

"It's me—Yamada, remember?" Shinji lied fluently. "I came once before—some time ago."

"Oh yes, of course, Mr. Yamada," she replied cheerfully, conducting him out of the lobby. These girls, he reflected, had congress with so many men each day, maybe over a hundred a month, so there was no question of remembering the face or name of a customer who had only come once some time ago.

Following her, he gazed at the sensuous nape of her neck and felt moved to erotic expectations. "Will you take a steam bath first?" she asked. What an extraordinary question, Shinji thought at first, and then reflected that some customers might be shy whilst others probably only did come here for the steam bath. He decided to play the role of someone who was shy or unromantic and opted for the bath. She led him to the cubicle, but instead of undressing, he killed time with questions.

"That customer you just had—his name is Seiji Tanikawa, isn't it?"

She was raising the lid of the steam chest, but she turned sharply toward him, a suspicious look on her face.

"Do you know him, then?"

"Well, it certainly looks like him, anyway. A bit embarrassing, bumping into him in a place like this."

"He's a regular of mine. Works for a film company, he says."

"Does he come here often?"

"Twice a week."

"He must be pretty well-off, then."

"Oh, I don't know. Maybe he makes money playing the stock market. Some of our customers come every day, you know. Maybe they're addicted to steam baths."

"I would say that that customer was more addicted to you."

She laughed and was not displeased. "Not really. He had another girl before me, but she left, so he switched to me. I came here to work just when the other girl quit, so he was handed over to me. A sheer fluke."

"I have heard a lot of people quit this job. Is it true?"

"Well, yes, I suppose you could say that in this business we have a high metabolism. As soon as a new place opens, everyone tries to join it for a better guarantee. People move a lot; I've been here six months, which makes me an old hand."

"Oh. Well, as Tanikawa is older than you, he must have been coming here for quite some time, I expect. When did he start, do you know?"

"Pretty recently, from what he has told me. He says he only came here once before meeting me, and that was a mere two days before, too. He says he went back to see the same girl again, but she had quit, so he switched to me. But men are full of stories, so I don't know."

"And when did you start work here?"

Again, the woman became cautious. In place of her merry chatter, she spoke somberly.

"You are investigating something, aren't you? Are you police, by any chance?"

152

"Do I look like a policeman? No, I've taken up divination recently," he extemporized quickly, "and the theme of my research is the causal relationship between a person's birthday and the day they take up any particular job."

"You can't fool me with that sort of tale. But if you want to know, my birthday is February sixth. And what day did I start working here? Just a moment." And she removed her handbag from the locker and extracted a notebook. "December twenty-first. And, oh my God, not one yen of tip that first day, I see."

"December twenty-first. Half a year."

"Yes, six months, and not a single day off. Every now and again I think of quitting this business," she added, and Shinji detected a look of desperation in her eyes. "But then I take a look at my bank book," she went on, "and my spirits soon recover, seeing it mounting up every day. When I reach my target, I'll quit and set myself up in something else."

She stood before him, and he looked at her chubby hands. Here she was, the innocent accomplice of men's desires. Those chubby hands . . .

And then it came home to him.

If the date she had given him was correct, and if Seiji Tanikawa had not lied to her, then the day of his first visit to the Turkish bath would have been the nineteenth of December. The day, in fact, that Fusako Aikawa had been killed!

Mere coincidence? Or was there some hidden meaning? In that steamy room, he felt cold sweat start to his brow.

"I must go!" he said rapidly. "I've just remembered something vital I promised to do! Sorry!"

"But what about your massage?"

"Some other time." And, grossly overtipping her, he fled.
If he was lucky, he might just catch Seiji Tanikawa in
some nearby small restaurant.

4

Shinji found Seiji Tanikawa in a low-class establishment
serving skewered chicken and beer. It stood in a narrow
street full of similar places, which ran down to the back of
the station. It was not the shop in the detective's report, and
Shinji was really very lucky to spot Tanikawa there, hunched
over the counter facing the street and wearing his black polo
shirt. When Shinji first saw him, he was inserting a skewer
into his mouth, the sauce dripping down his front. He
didn't even bother to look up when Shinji came in and sat
beside him. He was engrossed in his beer and chicken, and
when not occupied with them he would sit gazing blankly
into the middle distance.

"Hello, Mr. Tanikawa," said Shinji, and the man started,
spilling some of his beer.

"Nice to find you here!" Shinji continued.

"Who the hell are you?"

Shinji did not answer. Smiling in an obscure way, he
looked Tanikawa straight in the eye and said, "How are the
films doing, then?" As he spoke, he knew how a blackmailer

must feel, for he saw his victim's face darken and freeze as his words sank in.

"I said, who the hell are you?" Tanikawa finally spluttered.

It seemed that the reference to films had done the trick. Shinji took the pressman's business card out of his pocket and handed it over.

"A newspaperman, eh? What do you want with me? And what do you mean by 'films'?" He looked up from the card and stared at Shinji.

"Well, nothing in particular. I'd heard you work in the film-developing field, that's all. Today, my business is to inquire about blood donors. You cooperated in the Rh-negative collection campaign last year, didn't you? You won't remember me, perhaps, but I was there."

It was a shot in the dark, but it seemed to strike home. A look of relief gradually replaced the look of suspicion on Tanikawa's face. At least the reporter was not onto his blue film business.

"Can't say I remember, but maybe."

"Have you given blood since?"

"No, never."

"That's funny. Haven't the blood banks contacted you at all? I gathered from them that you gave blood in mid-January."

"Not me. Must have been someone else." His face was expressionless as he replied to Shinji's leading question. It did not look as if he was lying.

"Oh, I'm sorry—must have been our mistake." He had drawn a blank. Perhaps, after all, there were no fish in this pond in which he was dangling his rod. Or perhaps he had no bait, or even no hook, on the end of his line. He stood up to go.

"Hey, you're not going already, are you? Stay and drink a bit."

Shinji looked down at him. The man's speech was slurred and his eyes were red; alcohol was beginning to tell. What a bore! But he was in no hurry to go anywhere else, so he might as well stay a while. The image of the back of the pudgy white hands of the bath girl floated before his eyes; he'd better have a few drinks and forget them.

"O.K., I'll stay and join you." And he sat down again.

"My round," said Tanikawa magnanimously, and shouted for beer.

"Do you come here often?" asked Shinji, as much to make conversation as anything else.

"No, not really. I go to a Turkish bathhouse down the road."

"Sounds fun. Any nice girls there?"

At first, Tanikawa did not answer. He raised his beer mug up to the level of his eyes and gazed through the amber liquor. And then, watching the rising bubbles, he began to speak in tones of self-hatred.

"I see a girl there called Yasue every three days. And damn all good it does me. No love or anything about it—purely a commercial transaction. You can buy anything with money, you know. And I know it, too, but somehow I'm unable to

156

stop myself any more. I think I'm scared to stop; at least my life has some pattern the way things are. I am just a bloody fool!"

He was close to tears. He took a deep gulp of beer and went on.

"And it all started with one woman—it was her fault; do you understand me? Damn it! How cynical, how ludicrous life is! Look, I never went near a place like that until the end of last year! And there's a date I can never forget—December seventeenth last year. It was my day off; I went down to Kabukicho in Shinjuku and saw a film and then went into a cheap bar. That's where I met the woman; that's where she came and sat next to me and spoke to me . . ." His head suddenly slumped forward, sending his glass spinning into the ashtray, which fell to the floor and shattered. The spilled beer spread over the counter and started to drip down.

"Let me take you somewhere else," said Shinji hastily. He lifted the drunk man in his arms and, staggering under the dead weight, paid the bill and made his way outside.

Who could this woman be that Tanikawa had suddenly mentioned? Could there be anything to it? In the recesses of his brain, an indistinct female form took shape.

He staggered down the street, supporting Tanikawa, who was no help, but merely muttered again and again, "It was that woman, that woman . . ." Anything else he said was unclear.

Shinji hailed a taxi and dumped Tanikawa in the back, sitting beside him. "Mitaka!" he said. Tanikawa spread himself out so that his hair, which reeked of pomade, came close to Shinji's nose, and put his feet on the white covers of the seat back in front of him. This displeased the driver, who told him to desist in sharp tones.

The car moved off. Shinji wound down the window so that the wind blew into Tanikawa's face and shook him by the shoulder.

"And what did you do next—you and the woman?"

"Well, she took me to a bar and stood me several drinks. Then she said she had to go, but she wanted to see me again soon."

"She paid for all the drinks? Or did you go dutch?"

"No, she paid for the lot. And when we parted she told me that she worked for a Turkish bath and would I come and see her? She promised me good service and gave me a piece of paper with the name and address of the bathhouse on it."

"Have you still got it?"

"Yes—I've always kept it. Here, have a look." And he delved into his wallet and finally fished out a scrap of paper. "There, if you don't believe me!" His voice and his motions betrayed his drunkenness. Shinji took the paper and read it.

"Be sure to come at 9 P.M. the day after tomorrow. Don't forget—I'll be waiting for you. Kyoko." It was written in pencil but was still legible. Down the side, she had drawn a crude map showing the way to Alibaba.

Nine P.M. on the nineteenth of December last. Another coincidence? Looking at the paper, he was reminded of the printed messages that call girls leave on parked cars—name, telephone number, and some message such as: "Lonely to-night? Give me a ring."

"So you went there?" He handed the scrap of paper back to Tanikawa.

"Of course I did. And it was marvelous. You should have seen how she performed! And like a bloody fool, I thought she was interested in me! Why, she even refused a tip! She just said, 'Please come again.' So I went back the next day, but she was gone." He screwed the slip of paper into a ball and hurled it onto the floor of the car.

"What kind of a woman was she?"

"Oh, she was nice! And how she gazed at me with her large eyes with their double lids! It was enough to make you swoon!"

"Big eyes; double eyelids. Was that all? Was there nothing else special about her? So that you could recognize her again, I mean."

"Oh yes, she had a big mole at the base of her nose. It was really sexy! Could you really find her for me?" he cried in a maudlin fashion and then slumped over Shinji's knees and began to snore.

Shinji picked the ball of paper up off the floor and slipped it into his pocket. The car turned off the Koshu Kaido and into the Suido-doro.

Who could that woman have been? She had stood drinks to a stranger in a bar; although a Turkish bath girl, she turned down a tip. And then she vanished into thin air. Why? What had she been up to?

Ahead, the road, illuminated in the headlights of the car, seemed to rush toward him. He had better report this to the old man as quickly as possible. The car swung left down the edge of Inokashira Natural Park, whose thick groves were the last remains of the forests that had once covered Tokyo, and then turned down a gravel path that ran along the edge of the Mitaka Brook. Soon he would be there.

He would drop the drunk off, and then go to the apartment of Sada, the cosmetics salesman.

It was on his way, anyhow.

5

The coffee shop, Dakko, was located at the end of a shopping arcade. It was a tiny place built on the corner of the row, having no more than two box seats; five customers would be enough to fill it, and tonight it was overfull with men wearing clogs and light cotton kimonos who seemed to have nowhere in particular to go. A glance at the towels and soap containers that they all were holding revealed that they were all on their way back home from the public bath. Amongst this group, one man stood out, for he was wearing a summer suit and was tall for a Japanese—at least five feet seven. When Shinji entered, he spotted him immediately, for he seemed to be talking to himself, moving his large limbs in an exaggerated manner the while. He seemed to be rehearsing a sales pitch, and his soft, well-modulated voice betrayed him for what he was—a cosmetics salesman who made his living from women. The moment Shinji opened the door, their eyes met. Sada came over to Shinji, glancing at him shrewdly, and they sat down together in a seat that had just become vacant. Sada bowed slightly.

"Hello. Sorry, but I forget your name."

Shinji handed him a reporter's card. "I went to your apartment, but your wife told me you would be here, so . . ."

"Yes, she phoned me and told me." Sada proffered his card, his face set with his business smile.

"Thanks for coming," he went on. "As you can see, I'm ready for business twenty-four hours a day." He oozed politeness.

"Well, to be honest, it isn't that. I came in search of facts on blood donation. Have you given recently?"

"Well, there's been no call for it for quite some time. Rather a waste really—I'm a full-blooded fellow and have more than I need." Sada laughed at his weak joke.

"What about the fifteenth of January last?" he said, mentioning the date of Mitsuko Kosugi's murder. But Sada assured him that he had not given blood for at least a year. It seemed that Shinji's visit was wasted, and he decided to leave. However, having come so far, perhaps he should question Sada a little on his private life. It seemed that Sada was a man who liked to talk, and he was awaiting Shinji's further questions, moistening his underlip the while.

"The nature of your business must bring you into contact with all sorts of people. Have you got any interesting stories to tell me?"

"Not really. My life is pretty dull, really."

"Honestly?"

"Yes. The life of a cosmetics salesman consists of wearing down shoe leather, no more. I know there are a lot of stories about us, but they are not true, at least not in my experience."

"What about the jewelry business, then?" Shinji only said this in a spirit of light sarcasm, but it struck home. Sada's slimy eyes, which bulged as if he suffered from Basedow's disease, suddenly ceased their motion. He lowered his voice and leaned toward Shinji, plainly anxious not to be overheard.

"Detective, are you? I know what you are talking about, but we can't speak here, so let's move on somewhere else. There's a sushi shop called 'Kawagen' a few doors up; go and wait for me there." His tone was friendly but insistent.

Shinji decided to fall in with his plans. Leaving his coffee more or less untasted, he went out of Dakko.

He was sitting at the counter of Kawagen, wiping his hands with a cold flannel, when Sada came in. "Sorry to keep you waiting." He gave a few orders to the cook behind the counter and turned to Shinji again. "I had quite a difficult time with the lady, and it really wasn't my fault," he began.

"Go on," said Shinji, his curiosity aroused.

"Well, she rang me at home—must have got my number from another customer, I suppose. Anyway, she said she wanted to see some jewelry. Well, it's only a side business of mine, you understand, but anything to oblige.... Anyway, she said she wanted to see some jewelry and asked me to meet her at a coffee shop downtown. So, as I said, what the customer wants is always right, and I went to see a fellow I know who lets me have stock on consignment when I need it."

At this point, he broke off and ordered a tuna sushi, offering one to Shinji, too.

"Well, I went to the coffee shop, but on the way I had second thoughts. I mean, I was carrying a small fortune in gems, and I didn't know the woman from Adam. What if I was drugged and robbed? So I put my briefcase in a station locker and just took two pieces with me—the cheapest diamond in the batch and an opal. Why did I go at all in that case, you may ask. Well, there was something suggestive in the woman's manner that attracted me. Anyway, I got to the coffee shop in Yurakucho and there she was, waiting for me, wearing a kimono. Quite a beauty, and immaculately turned out.

"I was going to show her the jewelry, but she said the coffee shop was too public. We ought to go somewhere very private, she said to me archly, and I began to feel I wouldn't mind being cheated out of my jewelry if she would first give me a little bit of pleasure in return. As I say, she was beautiful. Anyway, we went to an inn in Sendagaya by taxi. When we got there, it was still before noon, but there were several other couples there already. It seems that those places have business twenty-four hours a day, you know. Makes you think, doesn't it?"

He paused to wolf down two sushi; looking at him, Shinji reflected that here was a man whose mouth never stopped moving, either in eating or in speech.

"So we went into a bedroom and she asked to see the jewelry. She said she liked both pieces and asked how much they were. Well, I was a little confused, so I quoted her a good price and she bought them both on the spot—and paid cash there and then, too." He laughed hollowly. "Well, we'd paid for the room for two hours, and it seemed a waste not to use it, if you see what I mean, and she was willing, it seemed. So we drank a little beer, and undressed, and then . . ."

"Yes?"

"And then nothing. I woke up and was lying on the bed all by myself. I called the front desk on the phone and they told me the lady had left an hour and a half before. That put the wind up in me, and I checked to see if anything was missing, but nothing was. Even the eighty thousand yen she had paid me for the jewelry was still there. It was just as if I had been possessed by a fairy or a ghost. But my head was strangely heavy and my throat dry, so I went back home and slept it off. Beer doesn't normally affect me like that; if you ask me, it was drugged. Anyway, that wasn't the end of it. The next day, when I returned the remainder of the jewelry to my friend, I discovered that the diamond I had sold her was a fake. Look, it's only a sideline of mine, and I'm no expert. I assure you that I had no intention of cheating her. Please believe me." He paused for a drink.

"Oh, yes, the money is quite intact—I've kept it in an envelope so as to give it back to her in due course. I've tried to track her down, but to no avail." The story was at an end, and he rounded it off with a laugh that seemed to Shinji to be extremely studied.

Was he telling the truth? Perhaps he had seen the incident as a small, illicit affair with a married woman and had taken the money without any qualms. But perhaps the fraud had been deliberate, and he was now making up this story to cover up his deceit. In either case, how could this bizarre tale be related to the case of Ichiro Honda?

"And when did this take place?"

"Let me see—I can tell you exactly." The salesman took a small notebook out of his breast pocket and examined it. "January fourteenth," he said.

The day before Mitsuko Kosugi was killed . . . but could there be any connection? Surely not. Feeling disappointed, Shinji poured himself a mug of green tea to take the taste of sushi out of his mouth. He prepared to leave, but the salesman began to speak again.

"Look, as I've told you, I'll give the money back. And to make amends, I'll give her some of the new cream I've got that covers up spots, freckles, and even moles. It contains ingredients imported from France and is rather expensive, but I will give her a jar for nothing."

Shinji listened in stunned silence.

"You know, that mole she has on the side of her nose."

Shinji absently picked up a small pebble that was lying on the counter and hurled it somewhere without particularly caring. It struck something, rattling hollowly.

"Yes, she was concealing it behind a handkerchief, you know, but of course that attracts more attention than if you are open about it. A mole isn't such a defect that you have to hide it; indeed, if displayed openly, it has a charm of its own. But this new makeup will take care of it." Sada chatted on, but Shinji sensed behind the self-confident charm of the salesman a deep concern about the money and the jewelry.

"What will happen as a result of all this?" Sada asked.

"Depending on how it turns out, you may have to give evidence in court. However, I don't think there's any way you will get into trouble over this. For the time being, hang on to the money."

"Court? Do you mean a divorce court?"

"Something like that." He got up to leave and made as if to pay, but Sada restrained him, laying an oily hand, sticky with sweat, on his wrist. Shinji allowed him to pay, thanked him and left.

He set off on foot for Asagaya Station. What did it all mean? How could he organize the jumble of facts into a coherent picture? Everything seemed so disconnected. In the damp heat of the evening, he couldn't think straight. If only Hatanaka was with him; the old man would soon put the pieces of the jigsaw together.

After all, he thought, he was just a reporter collecting facts and incidents for his master. He could almost see the old lawyer's heavy-lidded face, smell his fragrant cigar.

He reached Asagaya Station and bought a ticket to Shinjuku. Now for the last name on his list. He must go and talk to a boy in a homosexual bar.

He felt like going home to sleep instead but overcame the urge, as does a gambler who is determined to stay up all night.

6

The distance from Shinjuku Station to Hanazono-cho, which was where the gay bar was located, was quite far on foot. As Shinji headed in that direction, the majority of people were coming the other way. He collided with a hostess who was obviously in a rush to catch the last train, and she cursed him raucously.

Finally he came to Toden Avenue; crossing this broad thoroughfare and making his way toward the Hanazono Shrine, he finally came upon a maze of streets laid out like a gridiron behind the shrine, formerly an area licensed for prostitution. Turning into a narrow alleyway at the second intersection, he found himself in a jungle of tiny bars, each of them with a frontage no more than a few feet wide, and each advertising itself with a similar neon sign. There were also paper lanterns and painted boards; which, amongst these myriad establishments, could be his destination?

It was late, and the street was deserted. No voices of drunkards singing arose to assail his ears, as he might have expected. No heavily made-up woman tried to tug him into a doorway, as might normally be expected in such an area. He poked his head into a tiny bar occupied by a middle-aged woman in an apron and asked her how he could find his destination.

"I've no idea," she said. "Give up and have a drink here instead. I'll introduce you to a nice girl." She sat warming her feet over a charcoal brazier, which seemed to double as

an ashtray, so full was it of cigarette ends and broken chopsticks. He declined her offer and made his escape; after a few
moments he looked back, but there was no sign of her following him. It seemed that she was resigned to her lot and
no longer hustled for business.

Only one place showed any sign of life: a tiny restaurant
that had obviously once been a bar. From it wafted delicious
smells of fish on the grill and fermented bean soup. Shinji
suddenly realized that he had hardly eaten that night and
went in. Five customers would fill it; there were three—a
waiter off-duty, identifiable by his bow tie, and two tarts.
They looked up as he entered but betrayed no interest, soon
returning to their chopsticks and their bowls.

Behind the counter, an honest-looking couple in their
early fifties were working diligently; he took them to be
husband and wife. He glanced at the menu and ordered a
bowl of rice and salmon doused in hot tea. While it was
being prepared, he smoked a cigarette and reflected. The
faces of the four men that he had interviewed floated before
his eyes. The medical intern, the day laborer, the salaryman
at the film laboratory, the salesman of cosmetics . . . each face
rose before him in turn.

Of these four, two had nothing to tell him that he could
see was of any significance. The other two had both spoken
of the strange woman. And none of them had recently given
blood. Did that mean that they had no connection with
blood? If so, why had the person who had spoken to the
blood banks on the telephone been so interested in AB Rh-

negative? Surely he or she wanted to obtain some? Shinji was totally confused.

The cook brought his food, and he savored the perfumes of seaweed and sesame seed.

Just one more to go, he thought as he ate. The boy in the gay bar; was he the last stud card? Had he been turning up the wrong cards so far? It was almost like playing poker, he decided.

He ate the last mouthful and found it full of horseradish, which almost choked him. He gulped down some tea hurriedly and then asked the master the way to Bar B.

"It's right here—one floor up." The neon sign with the big letter B was under the eaves, he now realized, and he had not noticed it. He paid his bill, went out and began to climb the narrow staircase, which was so steep and contorted that he nearly fell halfway up. But upstairs turned out to be more spacious than he had expected; the room was occupied by four or five customers, all of them looking like pederasts. He flopped into a bar stool and hunched his shoulders. A boy with softly waved curls down his forehead came up to him.

"What can I get you, sir?"

"Beer," said Shinji.

"Yes, sir, of course, sir, please wait a moment," said the boy coquettishly and minced away.

Behind the counter were three other young men, all dressed identically in shirts with broad vertical stripes and narrow ties. They leaned on the counter flirting with the customers, occasionally stepping back and shaking their bodies sensuously in time to the music. They all wore tight jeans that were sculpted over their bottoms. And which of them could be Nobuya Mikami? Shinji had no idea, for although the detective agency had provided photographs of the other four men, they had omitted to do so in this case. Either the researcher was embarrassed to ask the precious young man for a photograph, or else he had presumed that Shinji would make contact by phone rather than visit the bar.

Perhaps it had been a mistake to come here, Shinji reflected as he sipped his beer; certainly his motives would be misunderstood. He put a cigarette in his mouth, and immediately the boy who had served him produced a light. There was a golden initial *A* embroidered on his tie.

"My name is Akiko," said the boy, pointing to the *A* on his tie. "How do you do?"

So they all had their initials on their ties, thought Shinji, and indeed it was so. Each boy had an initial on his tie, but none of them sported an *N*. Nobuya Mikami must be out with a customer. If he waited, would he be back?

"Is Nobu off tonight?" he asked.

"Oh, it's Nobu you want, is it? Sorry—he's out with a customer, taking a cup of tea together, if you see what I mean. Well, if you know him, you know how self-centered he is; he'll do anything, he says, if there's money in it for him!"

"Really," said Shinji. "A real pro, you mean?"

The boy giggled, but an epicene little man sitting at the counter next to Shinji turned to him, peered at him through his glasses and lisped, "Oh, my! I'm terribly sorry! Are you interested in Nobu, too? But do be careful—he's an awful tease, and quite cold-hearted. Why, once he went to a hotel to meet a strange man who phoned in, and the man gave him ten thousand yen, and still Nobu only spent an hour with him!"

"Wow!" said another customer. "What a boy! When was that?" Shinji found this intervention most convenient.

"Six months ago—on his birthday. You know, his best patron came and said, 'Let's celebrate in the grand manner. Tonight, everything is on me!' But as soon as that telephone call came, Nobu just walked out on us. 'An engagement,' he said, 'comes first.' Even Mama-san was disgusted with him that night! He came back after an hour and said, 'I had a steak in a hotel restaurant as I dissipated my energy.' What lies! Everyone knows hotel restaurants aren't open at that hour. Typical showing off! As if he'd buy a steak—he's too mean to give anyone even a sheet of tissue paper!"

"Some customer, to give him ten thousand yen. Wish I could find one like that!"

"But he only called the once, you know. Nobu hopes he'll call again, but he won't, mark my words. Once is enough with that cow! He's got no sense of service, that one, which is why all his customers leave him in the end."

It was Akiko, also known by the diminutive "Attchan," who was running down his rival behind his back. It appeared to Shinji that Nobu had stolen one of his customers off him. He sat listening to this and similar talk interspersed with suggestive banter between Attchan and the plump, pink customer on his right for thirty minutes, but still there was no sign of Nobu. Perhaps he'd better phone later. He paid his bill, a mere 350 yen for the beer and some tidbits, and left.

But when he got to the bottom of the stairs he found that it was raining outside. In fact, it was a downpour, and he decided to shelter there until it subsided. The water formed deep pools on the asphalt, reflecting the red neon light of the bar sign. He lit a cigarette and gazed at the furious deluge. Not a soul was in sight.

A taxi stopped at the end of the lane, and a man, his jacket pulled over his head, ran to where Shinji was sheltering. He paused under the eaves and put his jacket on; under it was a striped shirt, which revealed that he was a waiter from Bar B. He glanced at Shinji and smiled impishly. His face was feminine, with something of the soft roundness of childhood left in it. And on his tie was the intitial N.

"Nobu, I presume," said Shinji. "I have been waiting for you."

"Sorry to keep you waiting in this rain. Won't you come up?"

"No thanks—I spent quite a time there already. I must be on my way now—but just a question or two first." And taking a thousand-yen note out of his wallet, he folded it with deliberation and slipped it into Nobu's handkerchief pocket.

"I'm a lawyer," he went on. "I'm checking into blood donation. Have you given recently?"

"No."

"Are you sure?"

172

"Yes. I've become anemic of late. Are you looking for AB Rh-negative, then? What sort of operation is it for?"

Shinji just shook his head. His stud card had turned out to be useless after all; it was time for him to fold.

"Anyway," the young man continued, "I made a pledge at my last birthday that I would never give blood again. I make an important resolution every time I have a birthday. Who knows, next year I may resolve to quit gay bars!"

"And when is your birthday?"

"January fifteenth."

January 15 . . . the day that Mitsuko Kosugi was murdered. And the boy had said . . .

"And you said that something interesting happened to you on your birthday. What was it?"

"I didn't say it."

"Sorry, Attchan did."

"Oh. Well, it wasn't really anything nice—Attchan's jealous, that's all. I mean, yes, I was given money, but ooh, what a weird customer! I was called to the hotel by telephone. He made me take a bath, but he didn't remove a single garment—in fact, he even wore gloves throughout! A short guy, with a muffled sort of voice. And he only left a small bedside footlight on, so it was almost pitch dark. I don't think it's so romantic in the dark, do you?"

"And he gave you ten thousand yen?"

"That's right."

The rain had subsided; at the far end of the lane, a drunkard staggered along, supported by a harlot. And nobody had taken the boy's blood after all. So the old man's efforts—the careful listing of AB Rh-negative donors, his investigations with the blood banks—had been to no avail. His own long hours on the trail had also been useless.

"Thanks," he said weakly.

"Is that all you want of me?" said Nobu Mikami, winking at him lasciviously and tapping the handkerchief pocket into which Shinji had slipped the thousand yen. "But, between you and me, I think that all men with moles are a bit abnormal, don't you? My customer tonight had a large mole above his belly button, just where his fat was running to slack. Disgusting, I call it!"

The rain had at last stopped, and Shinji left without a word. But he had only gone a few paces down the narrow street before the significance of the boy's words struck home. He rushed back and caught Nobu halfway up the stairs.

"You said 'mole,' " he panted. "Do you mean that the customer on your birthday had a mole, too?"

"Sure—a big one on the base of his nose." He looked down the stairs at Shinji and laid his finger down one side of his nose suggestively.

"Are you sure the customer was a man? Could it not possibly have been a woman in disguise?"

The boy blinked in surprise at this peculiar question, but at length replied, "I have no idea—could be. I have lots of oddball customers, but it doesn't worry me so long as they pay. But if it was a woman, I don't know what on earth she wanted from me." He turned his back and vanished up the stairs, his full buttocks twinkling under the tight jeans.

Shinji stood there in stupefaction. At last it was all becoming clear.

Three out of the five people with that rare blood group had met someone with a mole on the side of his or her nose. But in every case the circumstances had differed. And, even more significant, those three meetings had occurred on the day of one of the murders or on the day before. Three moles on three noses, all connecting up in one line. It hadn't occurred to him until he had heard the boy's last words. But who could she be, this woman with a mole on her nose? What was she after? Question after question poured through his mind.

He hurried away from the shady quarter. On the main street, he looked for a public telephone.

7

He went into a coffee shop and used the public telephone to call up the old man at his home, but the maid answered and grumbled that he was not back yet. "And he didn't even say where he was going," she complained.

Where could he be, all by himself at this time of night? Shinji decided to wait a while for his return home and took a corner seat and ordered a cup of coffee. A few seats away, an avant-garde group of young people who seemed to be led by a young woman wearing white lipstick were striking extravagant poses and putting white tablets into their beer. Shinji ignored them. Getting his memo book out of his pocket instead, he began to write down his conclusions from his research to date:

1. *First murder.*   (*November 5*)
Kimiko Tsuda.
Nothing discovered relating to this day.

2. *Second murder.*   (*December 19*)
Fusako Aikawa.
On this day Seiji Tanikawa of the film-processing company first visited the Turkish bath at the behest of a woman with a mole on her nose.

3. *Third murder.*   (*January 15*)
Mitsuko Kosugi.
Nobuya Mikami (of the gay bar) was called on the phone and went out to a customer he had never met before. This customer, described as a man of short stature with a muffled voice, also had a mole on the nose.

4. *Event unknown.*   (*January 14*)
???????No murder case has been reported for this day.
On this day, the cosmetics salesman sold fake jewelry to a woman with whom he went to an inn at Sendagaya. This lady, who had the appearance of being a married woman, was smartly dressed in a kimono and also had a mole on her nose.

Common points concerning the person who appeared before the three witnesses are as follows:

1.   A fairly distinctive mole at the right side of the base of the nose.

2.   Only one appearance in each case before disappearing.

3.   Only approached men with blood of the AB Rh-negative group.

Shinji reread what he had written and contemplated. Although the gay boy had said that he had met a man, there was enough about his description to suggest that it could have been a woman in disguise. Above all, there was the mole.

So it was fair to assume that in all three cases, the person had been the same.

And it was highly likely that it was the same person who had telephoned the blood banks inquiring about the rare blood group.

So what lay behind this mysterious person's actions?

Why did she meet people with AB Rh-negative blood on the day of the murder, or the day before?

Suppose all three men had told the truth, and she had collected blood from none of them, what was her purpose behind these meetings?

She had always effected contact through sex.

So . . .

Perhaps her target was the semen, and not the blood, of the men! This seemed to Shinji to make sense.

A murderess . . . gathering secretions from the bodies of men . . . leaving them in the bodies of her victims . . . how morbid! If he were a psychopathologist, he might be able to explain the distortion of the criminal's mind, but as a lawyer he had no theories. His mind was horrified at the thought of this woman who gathered the sperm of men with clammy hands and then bent over the bodies of the women whom she had strangled. Could it really have been a woman, and not a man in disguise, who had entrapped Ichiro Honda?

He looked again at the list. There was no appearance noted on the first occasion, the murder of Kimiko Tsuda. Did he, or she, visit someone with this obscure blood group on that day, too? he wondered. If so, it had to be either the day laborer Oba or else Yamazaki, the medical intern. Which of them had lied to him?

By process of elimination, the day laborer seemed the most unlikely, particularly if the criminal was a woman. And then in his mind's eye he was again sitting in the Bluebird coffee shop, facing the pale face of Yamazaki. What had the man said in response to his questions about blood? "Blood is an old-fashioned topic." What had he meant? And then Shinji suddenly realized.

Had Yamazaki not spoken of an interview with a third-rate magazine . . . on the topic of artificial insemination? Was not this a hint? Had the woman with the mole also approached Yamazaki? What had transpired to link him, his blood group, the woman with the mole, and the case of Ichiro Honda?

Perhaps the sentencing of Honda to death had given him

a guilty conscience; perhaps this was why he had remained silent about . . . about what? About the giving of his sperm. Shinji felt sure that it was Yamazaki who could fill in the blank space in his notebook. He would visit him again at the hospital tomorrow.

He stirred his lukewarm coffee. One question remained in his mind. The cosmetics salesman had met the woman with the mole on the fourteenth of January. If he wasn't lying, and if the woman had not taken sperm from him, then what had she taken? The only possible answer would be blood.

When he was lying insensible on the bed, she had taken his blood.

That was it; that made sense. So the old man's theory that the criminal had taken blood from these men was correct! And his harvest today had been a woman with a mole on the base of her nose.

Suddenly he felt weary. He called the old man's home again, but still he was not back. He paid and left.

In the street, he suddenly thought of his empty apartment where no one was awaiting him. And by contrast, he thought of the plump, white hands of Yasue, the girl in the Turkish bath, and of the slim nape at the back of the neck of Michiko Ono as she had walked ahead of him in the damp-smelling library.

He shook his head to clear it of such thoughts and walked heavily toward the station.

The Black Stain

I

The waiting room near to the entrance of the hospital was crowded with outpatients with bandages on them and with mothers soothing fretful children. It was just after 9 A.M.—opening time. Shinji sat on a hard wooden bench waiting to see intern Yamazaki. A little girl with short, bobbed hair sitting next to him had just wiped her caramel-covered hands all over his trousers; the child's mother had said, "Don't do that!" absently, her eyes looking away at something else.

Yamazaki came in. Tall and elegant, he wore his white coat with distinction, one hand in the pocket, the front buttons undone. *Stylish fellow,* Shinji thought.

Shinji rose to greet him. "Thank you for seeing me yesterday."

"Not at all. But why are you back again today? I'm busy, you know."

"Yes, I do realize, but I won't keep you long. Look, I told

you I was a journalist, but that isn't true. I'm a lawyer." And he presented his genuine card. The intern gazed at it with interest.

"I'm defending Ichiro Honda. Incidentally, do you know his blood type?"

"Yes. I saw in the newspaper. It's the same as mine."

"We are convinced of his innocence. For one thing, we do not believe that the AB Rh-negative blood found under the fingernails of the victims was his. The same applies to the sperm that was found."

"Really? Are you implying that the blood was mine?"

"Not the blood. The sperm."

The intern was speechless for a moment; he stared at Shinji out of the corner of his eye and then broke into a high-pitched laugh that had a hollow and insincere ring. "Very interesting. And what makes you so sure?"

"Well, you told me yesterday that you were interviewed by a popular magazine on the topic of sperm donation. That's correct, isn't it? So you have some experience, don't you?"

"Well, yes, I'm one of several medical students here who donate. Usually about three of us, but sometimes four or five. But the names are always kept confidential, and even if you give you don't know if it will be used. But what on earth can this have to do with Ichiro Honda?"

"I have reason to believe that you donated on the fifth of November last year."

"Wait a minute." Yamazaki consulted his pocket diary.

He shook his head. "I didn't note it, and my memory of last year is hazy. I have a feeling that I donated in about October, but I can't be sure."

"And where would the donation have taken place?"

"Why, here, of course."

"And how is it usually collected?"

The faint smile vanished from Yamazaki's face. His susceptibilities were plainly offended. "I don't see why I have to go into details.... I don't see what bearing... Oh, very well, I suppose there's no harm in telling you. In a test tube, of course."

"So someone goes around collecting these tubes? For example, a nurse?"

"No, we usually hand it over to the registrar in person."

Whilst talking, they had moved away from the crowd and were now standing by a window next to a shoe locker. To the casual observer, they would have been seen as two men holding a light conversation.

"Look," said Shinji. "A man's life depends upon this. You won't have to go into court and give evidence if you don't want to, but please just tell me the truth. On or just before the fifth of November, did you not give a test tube of sperm to someone other than the registrar—even, a faint possibility that occurs to me, to a strange nurse?"

A cool breeze, chilled by the shade of the trees outside, blew in through the window. Kotaro Yamazaki had turned his back on Shinji, causing the latter to reflect on how such a gesture symbolizes rejection. After a pause, Yamazaki turned and faced Shinji again.

"How much do you think the hospital pays me?" His voice was low and challenging. Shinji did not reply.

"Nothing, that's the answer! No matter how long you've worked, nothing. You've got to be rich to become a doctor, you know! A lot of the others are themselves sons of doctors, so they can afford it and don't mind working like horses for nothing. I'm not complaining; that's the way it is. I'm just saying it's easier to qualify if you are rich, if you're a doctor's son like those others, so I ask you to spare a thought for people like me who have to make it on our own. Yes, I did sell a test tube of semen for ten thousand yen on the fifth of November last year, if you must know."

"Ten thousand yen! That's a lot of money! What's the normal rate?"

Yamazaki again turned his back on Shinji and answered over his shoulder. "A thousand or fifteen hundred." His voice seemed to be full of self-contempt.

"And what did the person look like—the one who came to collect the tube?"

"A nurse in a white uniform. It was in the afternoon, I think. I had just had lunch, and was walking down the corridor when a strange nurse carrying a test tube appeared and, having identified me, offered me ten times the usual rate to make an urgent donation under conditions of strict secrecy. I accepted without hesitation. I mean, ten thousand yen. And in other ways it was not such an unusual request."

The nurse had waited for him to make the donation and had then left. She had introduced herself as being from the K Obstetric Clinic in Setagaya.

"And you got the payment all right?"

"Oh, yes, she gave it to me in a brown envelope together with the test tube."

"And what did you do with the envelope?"

"I threw it away."

"Can you remember what she looked like?"

"Not particularly. A small woman in a nurse's uniform, which contributes to anonymity. When she turned to go, I saw that her hair was braided under her cap."

"Did she have a mole at the right base of her nose?"

Shinji touched his nose to refresh Yamazaki's memory.

"Yes, she did, now you mention it. Quite a big mole. She was wearing a mask at first, and I didn't see it."

So the woman with the mole had come here, too. She had collected semen; her criminal intent now seemed clear.

"And she took her mask off?"

"Yes. She apologized for having a cold and blew her nose. That's when she took the mask off and I saw the mole."

So she invariably tried to conceal the mole, and thereby drew attention to it. Was the criminal fighting a losing battle with fate?

"Did she give you the impression of being disguised?"

"Not at all. A white uniform in a hospital is most natural, after all, so I thought nothing of it."

"But didn't you think it a bit peculiar—coming from so far to collect semen?"

"Not really—she could have used a taxi."

"Do you usually keep donations so secret?"

"Our professor tells us to. And it's an important principle,

184

don't you agree? Can I go now? Frankly, by nature I don't like discussing things that are over and done with." His face had grown cold.

"Of course, and I'll treat everything you have said in strict confidence, don't you worry. But just one last question before you go. Yesterday, you told me that blood donation is a stale topic and that artificial insemination is more interesting. You even mentioned an interview with a popular magazine. Frankly, it seemed to me that you were being evasive. Now I want you to be perfectly frank with me. Did it not later occur to you that there was some connection between this incident and Ichiro Honda's case? Didn't there seem to be some linkage, perhaps more than coincidence, between the date of your donation and the rape-murder in Kinshi-cho?"

"No, not for one minute. Your hypothesis lacks scientific substance." He looked disdainfully at Shinji and went on. "Human beings are divided into secretory and nonsecretory types, you know. It is only in the case of a secretory type that the semen and saliva are identical in type to the blood. And I am a nonsecretory type. So although my blood type is AB, my semen and saliva will not show up as AB but as O. If you don't believe me, look it up or go and ask an expert."

"And how do you know you are nonsecretory? Most people wouldn't, would they?" Shinji made a last effort to catch him out.

"We were experimenting in the forensic lab at university, and they used a cigarette butt that I had smoked. Do you know that you can detect a saliva type from one-third of a postage stamp that someone has licked? So that's how I know." And without further ceremony he turned away from Shinji, hurrying down the corridor with long strides.

Could this really be true? Could the semen found in the body of Kimiko Tsuda not belong to Yamazaki after all? So was he wrong in his theory about the woman with a mole who collected samples of AB Rh-negative blood and sperm? His supposition, which had seemed to be 99 percent probable, seemed on the point of collapse. But then, why would the woman with the mole bother to collect Yamazaki's semen?

Shinji felt that he was still blundering in the dark.

2

Shinji came to the end of his report, but even then the old man did not raise his hooded eyes. He was gazing down at the scrap of paper that the Turkish bath girl had given to Tanikawa, tapping it absently with his fingertip. Was the old man silent because the case had turned out to be as he had expected? Was he stunned by this or merely satisfied? And yet, was there not an enormous hole in his theory—the matter of secretory and nonsecretory types, which Yamazaki had explained?

"The fact that Yamazaki is a nonsecretory type, and that his fluids are type O, does not matter at all," said Hatanaka at length. "Indeed, it only goes to prove that the woman with the mole did use his sperm."

"Why?"

"Well, go back and read the trial transcript. You will find that the semen found in Kimiko Tsuda's body was originally classified as type O. However, a later submission by the prosecution to have it reclassified AB was upheld by the judge. It was partly due to this doubt that Honda was acquitted of that murder. However, it now seems plain to me that the original assessment was correct and that the semen found in the corpse must have indeed been type O."

"But surely it is a matter of scientific fact rather than surmise?"

"Not a bit of it. Expert evidence is often just as subjective as lay evidence. Two different professors are quite likely to come up with two different views."

"So you are convinced that the woman with the mole is the person who entrapped Ichiro Honda?"

"Can there be any doubt? I am quite convinced that the woman with the mole collected the semen and deposited it in the women's bodies. And furthermore, I have proof that these crimes were premeditated for a long time. You see, last night I went to a bar called Boi in Shinjuku." The old man's eyes were like curtains; he paused and lit a fresh cigar.

"Let me tell you a little story. One summer's evening just two years ago, Ichiro Honda was in that bar, singing the 'Zigeunerliedchen.' A girl joined him and sang with him. And they ended up spending the night together."

"Where did they go? An inn?"

"Probably, but it is not relevant."

Shinji felt the excitement welling up inside him; at the same time, he felt disgusted by Honda's promiscuity.

"And let me tell you another little story. Six months later, there was a key-punch operator who took her own life; she fell from the window of an office building." He drew heavily upon his cigar, blowing the purple cloud of smoke high toward the ceiling. "And the two stories are linked, for the girl was the same in each case. The girl who killed herself, and the girl who slept with Honda after singing 'Zigeunerliedchen.' One and the same—Keiko Obana, aged nineteen."

"And was Honda the cause of her suicide?"

"No. She had become neurotic because of a vocational disease." Shinji was listening attentively, but in place of the key-punch operator he was thinking of his former lover, the lending clerk in the library. She, too, had slept with Ichiro Honda, hadn't she? He reflected bitterly upon his client.

Somewhere in the distance, he heard the old man continue. "Keiko Obana had an only sister, much older than she was." Hatanaka's voice was like a bee heard at a distance in a summer garden. "When Honda told me about Keiko Obana yesterday, I felt I had to go to the bar. So I went and sat in the box seat on the second floor where Honda said the girl was sitting before the singing began. After a little while, I heard the weeping strains of a violin from the ground floor, just as Honda had described to me. So I sent for the player and asked him to play 'Zigeunerliedchen.' The violinist, a bald old man, changed his expression sharply at my request."

At last Hatanaka opened his sleepy eyelids and gazed at his

junior. The old man's voice began to take on an urgency that Shinji had never heard before.

"The player grinned at me in a crooked way and remarked, 'Customers at Boi certainly like this song, don't they, sir?' I asked him what he meant, and he looked knowing and replied, 'Next you are going to tell me that a thin girl occupied this seat and sang in chorus with a man downstairs. That would be right, wouldn't it, sir?'" The old man stubbed out his cigar. "I asked if anyone else had put these questions to him, and he immediately answered that a woman had, about a year ago."

Shinji felt as if he had suddenly been pulled from a dark coalhole into brilliant sunshine. He watched the old man's lips as a gambler watches the dealer; it was as if two cards were about to be turned up, and they would both turn out to be the same.

"So I asked what the woman looked like. All he could remember was that she had a mole at the base of her nose, for the rest of her face was concealed by a wide-brimmed hat and sunglasses."

Silence dominated the room. What had that woman with the mole been up to? Surely, Shinji thought, the old man was right; she was preparing to entrap Ichiro Honda.

"And what did the woman ask of the violinist?"

"The name of the man who had sung in union with the girl, and also the bars that he frequented."

"And that was a year ago?"

"Yes. Just four months before the murder of Kimiko Tsuda at Kinshicho."

"And who do you think she was?"

"I don't know, but I have my suspicions. A relative of Keiko Obana's, I'd say."

"And the sister was the only relative?"

"Yes. I read up all the newspaper articles that came out at the time of the suicide. They were living together in an apartment at Omori. So I've sent a researcher off there to see what he can find."

Shinji drew in his breath sharply, an involuntary sign of respect. The Hatanaka Law Office had found the trail, which would help it in its efforts to defend Ichiro Honda. It did indeed seem as if there was some connection between the key-puncher's suicide and the murders. He saw in his mind's eye those three faces: the worker at the film laboratory, the cosmetics salesman, the homosexual prostitute. Now they had to string together the moist episodes in the secret lives of these three men of a rare blood group and so prove Honda's innocence.

The old man had again closed his eyes as if in sleep. Suddenly the phone on his desk rang with heart-stopping suddenness; the old man was shaken, for his hands trembled as he picked up the receiver.

The conversation was one-sided; occasionally, the old man would grunt or interject a terse word. Meanwhile, his right hand was engaged in scribbling on the memo pad in front of him. He replaced the receiver and lay back with his eyes closed, and Shinji knew better than to interrupt. After a while, the old man opened his eyes, lit a cigar and spoke.

"Keiko Obana's sister moved from the Omori apartment

last September. No one knows where she went, just that she moved. But all the people living around there describe her in the same way—a woman with a large mole on the right-hand side of her nose."

"So that's it; we've got her, haven't we?"

"No. In addition to finding her, we've got to find a motive, and also how the crimes were committed." The old man showed his normal prudence.

"She must have believed that her sister killed herself because of Honda deserting her."

"I expect so."

"So we must find out where the sister is."

"That may not be so easy. However, I agree with you that we have no alternative." The old man's voice was suddenly tired, and Shinji could see why. A person capable of the cunning that had been used to trap Ichiro Honda would be no less capable of disappearing from the face of the earth once the plot was complete. If they failed to prove Honda's innocence, and if he were executed, would the real criminal wallow in secret satisfaction? Or would he or she—and it seemed to be she—have killed herself by then?

The old man looked up at Shinji. "I'd like you to go to the police station that handled Keiko Obana's suicide," he said, half apologetically.

3

The M Police Station was housed in a gray building so dirty in color as to be almost sordid. Shinji reported to the policeman at the front desk and was kept waiting on a plain wooden bench in the entrance hall for some time. The section chief who had been in charge of Keiko Obana's case was informing the relatives of the discovery of a drowned corpse in the palace moat that morning. Eventually he came out, conducting a matronly looking woman whose eyes were red from weeping. She had a small baby on her back, poor soul, and Shinji reflected that those who are left behind always suffer most.

The section chief greeted him amiably and conducted him into his room. But when he heard that Shinji's business concerned Keiko Obana, his face set in firm lines and he crossed his arms.

"It is correct that this station handled the suicide of Keiko Obana, a key-punch operator with K Life Insurance. We officially decided that the motive for suicide was neurosis caused by a vocational disease." As he spoke, his eyes avoided Shinji's; he stared at the wall or else widely over his shoulders, as if addressing a large audience. Shinji judged him to be an honest man who did not like telling lies.

"Yes, that's very interesting, but apart from the official version, what else can you tell me—off the record, of course." The section chief struggled with himself for a moment and then obviously decided there was nothing for it but to tell the truth.

"Well, there's one thing I did not make public, and that was on my own responsibility. Keiko Obana was six months pregnant at the time of her death. I did not tell the press, and I hope you see why."

192

"Did you tell anybody?"

"Just her sister, when she came to collect the body."

"And did she know who the child's father was?"

"It seems that it was some man that she met at an all-night café or some such place." But it was so long ago that the policeman did not wish to talk further without reference to his records and, excusing himself, went over to the filing cabinet in the corner of the room. Shinji gazed at the toe caps of his shoes and reflected, *So Keiko Obana, too, was pregnant by Honda.* That would surely give Keiko Obana's sister adequate motive for revenge. How many people would pardon such a thing? How many more would never forgive?

He imagined the sister sitting in this room, perhaps in this very chair, two years ago and hearing the news of her dead sister's pregnancy. Did she not at that moment fix her mind upon revenge? And after so many long nights, so many slow dawns, would she ever have relented? Perhaps grudges bring out the most tenacious in the human spirit.

The policeman came back to his desk, bearing a file. Shinji hastened to ask him the most important question that was on his mind.

"Did the sister have a mole on the right side of her nose?"

"Oh, yes, a big mole—I remember it quite clearly, although I forget which side it was on."

"And did she seem very shocked to learn that her sister was pregnant?"

"To the extent that I felt pity when I saw her reaction and half wished that I had not told her. And I am quite accustomed in my duty to imparting bad news to the relatives of suicides and witnessing their grief."

Shinji half thought of observing that the sister must have been indeed a beautiful woman to have won the sympathy of the section chief, but he thought better of it.

He glanced quickly through the file and, thanking the section chief, left the building. He wondered if he could bring out what he had learned in court; it would certainly put the policeman in a difficult spot for having covered up the pregnancy out of the kindness of his heart.

The lives of men and women are like toothed cogs; once one cog slips out of sync, it damages not merely those around it but also others having no direct connection with it. Thus, now, the tiniest secrets of individuals were likely to be laid before the public gaze. Not just the policeman—the cosmetics salesman and the medical intern, too.

He phoned the office and reported the results of his visit to the police station, but the old man did not seem in the slightest surprised. "Is that so?" was his only response.

"Well, I'll be off to check out the Omori apartment," Shinji said and hung up. He must do his best to track down Keiko Obana's sister as quickly as possible.

The apartment was located close to the waterfront, and he could smell the sea as he got out of the taxi. "It's somewhere round here," the driver said and was of no further assistance. He had to hunt for the red pillar box that stood on the corner near the building. When at last he found it, it proved to be a cheaply constructed wooden edifice, its corridors cluttered with such junk as old earthen braziers, empty orange boxes, and so forth.

He found a housewife roasting fish over a charcoal brazier, which she had taken into the garden. She seemed to be a person who liked to talk and answered him immediately. Fortuitously, it turned out that she lived immediately next door to Number 5, which was where the Obana sisters had lived. The surviving sister had moved out in the last September. The decision had apparently been very sudden, and she had sold all her furniture to the local secondhand shop. She had let it be known that she was moving to the west of Japan and had departed without making the appropriate round of farewell calls.

"Did she have any visitors just before she left?"

"I heard that a journalist from a woman's magazine came to interview her about her sister's suicide two or three times, but I don't think she had any other visitors."

"So no one knows where she went?"

"Well, she did talk about going back to Hiroshima sometimes, but . . ."

"Did she use a removal firm when she left?"

"No, I doubt it. There was nothing to carry—she even sold her bedding. But she left late at night, so none of us saw her go. The rumor is that she got paid a lot of condolence money for her sister's suicide, and so she probably went home and set herself up in some small business."

He thanked her for her help and left. He could not help feeling gloomy, for it was clear to him that tracking down Keiko Obana's sister would be no easy task. Suppose—and it seemed quite possible—that she had vanished on purpose; how could he find her amongst over one hundred million Japanese? And there was a deadline—the opening day of the trial at the appeal court. And that was looking on the bright side of things, presuming that she was still alive. What if she had killed herself—had plunged into the crater of an active volcano, or cast herself into a whirlpool, had gone, in fact, where none would ever find her body? Such cases were common enough.

He was caught in a steel trap, and the more he moved, the more hopeless his predicament became. In the taxi, he decided to make inquiries at the various scenic spots where people commit suicide. One never knew, after all . . .

He got back to the office, but the old man was out. The secretary, Mutsuko Fujitsubo, was engaged in copying a newspaper advertisement.

"Mr. Hatanaka has gone to the prison. He asked me to place an advertisement in the missing-persons section of the paper—do you think that this will do?" And she handed him her draft.

MISSING PERSON.

TSUNEKO OBANA. Aged 31. Born in Hiroshima city. Lived at Fujii Apartment, Sansei-cho, Omori-kaigan, Shinagawa-ku, Tokyo, until last September. Distinctive feature: a large mole, about the size of an Azuki bean, on the right base of her nose.

We wish to contact her urgently. A reward will be paid for information leading to her whereabouts.

HATANAKA LAW OFFICE

"Did Mr. Hatanaka tell you to publish this every day?"

"Yes, for at least a month."

"Pity we haven't got a photo."

"That's what Mr. Hatanaka says. He says we might be led on a wild-goose chase and end up with the wrong person."

Shinji went over to the window and looked down on the park below. The pigeons that congregated every morning on the windowsill were gone about their noonday business. There was a delicate haze over the woods of the park; the sky above was scattered with cumuli. Somehow or other, he thought, they would not track down Keiko Obana's sister. She had vanished, and it was due to the crimes.

His premonitions, dark as winter, contrasted with the vigorous skies of summer outside.

Insertion

A Monologue

The woman stretched her hand slowly to the pillow on the bed where she lay. These noises in her head; she must calm them.

Her lean hand looked like a dehydrated chicken leg: no flesh, only skin and bones.

That dry hand clawed under the pillow and took out a large notebook. The cover was soiled, with inky fingerprints showing on certain parts.

On the cover were brushed the words "The Huntsman's Log." But the word *Huntsman* was so stained as to be almost illegible. It had been read so often . . . it sent away, for a while, the noises in her head.

She brought the notebook to her breast. After a while, she opened it and flipped the pages, stopping at the tenth page. Her eyes were concave, like black holes drilled in her head, like the eyes of a rotting corpse. Just visible in the dark hollows were muddy pupils, which no longer seemed to focus.

The lean hand flipped the pages precisely, but the eyes did not seem to see. This was her daily routine, so most of the words in the diary were inscribed in her heart. Her hand came to rest at a certain page.

Prey had a strong head for drink. Anyway, no resistance, no hysterics, no overacting. Just put herself into my hands. Felt like a god accepting a human sacrifice.

Did her best to satisfy my every need, but was too tense and kept trembling. Took two hours to kill. She was a virgin; drew blood.

"Silly, silly little girl. Don't say you cried in his arms; don't tell me that you were crushed under his body. Don't try and tell me any of those things. I bet you were biting your lip with those sharp little teeth of yours that you always kept so clean; I bet you bit so hard that the blood came. Silly little girl!

"Silly to shed blood for his enjoyment! That man, to steal two hours of pleasure, pressed his filthy lips against your girlish and unsullied skin. He left his sticky seed of sin within your childlike body, not yet mature, and all for his own selfish satisfaction! Was it in spite of that seed, or was it because of it, that seed growing in your body, that you were forced to die? And as you were preparing to kill yourself, that man had long forgotten you and was tasting the flesh of some other woman. . . . But it's all right now, darling; don't cry any more. Curse him no more, though you lie underground being eaten by worms!

"For I have taken revenge, in spite of these sounds in my head. I have put him away into prison, where he can never touch any woman's body again. Now he faces the hard wall of a cold cell, doubtless inscribing upon it your name, yours and the names of many other women, with his anecdotes of those nights spent together. Soon, they will take him away and hang him, and then they will place a heavy tombstone above him. It will press down upon him firmly so he won't be able to budge an inch ever again. So there! Instead of pressing himself upon your body, upon the bodies of other women, the stone will press him! Cruel stone, press him!

"Now let me tell you how I made that man taste the same agony with which he fed you. . . ."

The Black Stain—Continued

I

A week passed after the advertisement was placed in the newspaper, and many leads came about Tsuneko Obana, but all of them were false trails. And then there came the first real clue. It was from the manager of an apartment building called the Midori-so, the building where Mitsuko Kosugi was murdered. He reported that a woman with a mole on the right side of her nose had been residing there under the name Keiko Obana since last September.

The woman was a little over thirty and worked as a model for a cosmetics company. This work took her to department stores the length and breadth of Japan, so she only spent about two days a week in the apartment. And for the last two months, she had not shown up at all.

"Well, she'd paid six months in advance, so at first I thought nothing of it. But recently I got worried and was thinking of going to the police, when I saw your advertisement."

The manager, who had the air of a war veteran, talked in

tones that bespoke his honesty. His linen suit, shiny with age, was well pressed and stank of mothballs; obviously, it was only worn on special occasions. The mole, the age, the recent disappearance . . . all added up to the elusive Tsuneko Obana.

"Right under our noses, so we didn't see it!" Shinji exclaimed. The old man said nothing, and Shinji then reflected that there was something fishy; why use Keiko Obana's name? Wasn't that a giveaway?

The old man seemed to be thinking the same thing; he chewed his cigar in a perplexed manner.

"Let us suppose that the woman really is Tsuneko Obana, as seems likely," he said. "Then it seems that she used her sister's name to make clear her intention of revenging her sister. In that case, we can presume that she has vanished again, this time perhaps for good."

At all events, they decided to visit the apartment immediately. The old man sent for his secretary and told her to give the manager the reward, which was handed over in a brown paper envelope, the manager protesting politely at first. A hire car was called, and soon they reached the Midori-so at Asagaya. Until they arrived there, the old man spoke not one word but merely pondered, chewing his cigar the while.

First of all, they looked into Mitsuko Kosugi's room. In spite of the housing shortage, no one had moved in—naturally enough, in view of the fact that somebody had been murdered there. Both the door and the windows stood open, as if to wash out some half-sensed odor of the mortuary.

There was nothing to see, so they went upstairs to the Obana room.

It was very neat and tidy. The manager, half-fearfully, opened the door of the closet, but it proved to contain no more than a set of bedding. All seemed in order, and yet Shinji felt strangely uncomfortable. Why did the woman with a mole rent this apartment under the name of a dead woman? Why had she now abandoned it? He thought of hermit crabs moving from shell to shell; had she not thus, once more, effected her escape? Would she ever return? Where was she now?

A deep sense of disappointment suffused his body and mind.

He went to the window and looked out. The street below, with its stepping-stones set in the mud, looked commonplace and dirty by the light of day. But at night, in the dark, would it not become the theater of horror from which Ichiro Honda had stumbled?

The old man called him, and he turned and went over to the low Japanese table where Hatanaka was standing. The drawer was open, and the old man was pointing at a large notebook that lay within. Shinji's body tensed with a thrill similar to vertigo.

"The Huntsman's Log!" he breathed.

"Yes," said the old man, turning the pages quickly, staring at them myopically through his thick glasses. "But the passage about Keiko Obana has been removed." He showed Shinji where the pages had been violently torn out.

"Did you find something?" asked the manager.

"This," said the old lawyer, quickly slipping it into his pocket. "And I'm going to keep it as evidence." On such occasions, Hatanaka was adept at glossing over the boundary between the requirements of the law and of reality.

Impressing upon the manager the need to contact them immediately if Obana showed up, they left the Midori-so. In the car, Shinji broke the silence.

"Will she come back?"

The old man shook his head. "I don't think so. The bird has flown, all right. She left the Huntsman's Log deliberately, just for someone like us to find if we could." He began to read the diary with care, Shinji peering over his shoulder.

He saw the passage referring to Michiko Ono, the librarian, and he felt a stabbing pain in his heart. He turned away and gazed out of the window.

The town lay in the dust of a summer's afternoon. The air conditioner of the car was blowing on his neck, no matter how he moved. They passed Shinjuku Station; some construction work was going on in the forecourt, and there was a temporary wooden sidewalk laid, over which the crowds moved slowly through the summer heat. Dump trucks came and went, dropping piles of earth onto the road.

Of what avail had it been for him to visit men with Rh-negative blood and to track down the woman with the mole? Was he not, in spite of it all, no more than a bystander? The real protagonists—Ichiro Honda, Michiko Ono, the woman with the mole, the murdered women, even—they had gone to the edge and looked down into the depths of life, and in some cases had returned. He had been nowhere. He had watched from the outside.

The old man was still buried in the diary. He looked up, beaming. "He really has got a good memory!" he exclaimed. "His reconstruction was almost perfect, even down to the order of things!" He turned the pages again, and suddenly his face stiffened.

"But there's a page missing at the very front—look, can you see where it has been torn out?" It was true.

"Who did he say his first victim was? Surely it was . . . Yes, it's the woman who appears as number two in this book. But there was obviously somebody before her—who could it have been? And why is the page missing?"

The old man closed his heavy eyelids and began to think. Eventually he spoke, half to himself.

"If we are not careful, we are in danger of making a big mistake."

He spoke with pain; had he suddenly realized some mistake that he had already made in his theorizing? Shinji tried to engage him in conversation as the car rolled through the town, but to no avail. When the car stopped at a red light at Hibiya, the old man broke his silence; leaning forward, he said to the driver, "Sugamo Prison, please."

On the way to the jail, Shinji's mind was in a turmoil. He longed to read the Huntsman's Log, which was reposing on the old man's knee, and yet he half dreaded the thought. What had Honda written about his affair with Michiko

Ono? How fully did he describe his lovemaking? In what tones had Michiko spoken to him? He realized that he was jealous.

For him, curiosity about his old lover meant as much as the torn-out page in the diary meant to the old man.

2

The waiting room at the prison was hot and stuffy; Shinji's face ran with sweat. The old man sat steady as a rock, his black bag, containing the diary, on his knee. At last their turn came, and they went into the interview room.

The condemned man naturally wore no necktie, and this added to his appearance of shabbiness and depression. Just as the old man had said, he looked as if all the fight was gone from him. He was in need of a shave, and his hair was dry and disheveled. And above all, the light was gone from his eyes.

Was this the man who had held Michiko Ono close to his breast? Shinji realized that he was glaring at Honda and quickly adjusted his countenance to one of total unconcern—unconcern toward Honda, toward the stone walls and the flagged floor.

"We have found the diary," said the old man. Behind the wire netting, Ichiro Honda was momentarily speechless.

"Where?" he said at last, his lips twitching. His deep voice was somber.

"At the Midori-so, where Mitsuko Kosugi was murdered. Obana's sister had an apartment on the second floor of the same building. We had advertised for her, and the manager of the apartment came to see us today. She moved in there in September, but hasn't been near the place for the last two months."

"I see," said Honda, hanging his head low, his hands joined loosely between his knees. "Now I understand. When I went there, I noticed the name 'Obana' on a shoe box at the entrance, but I didn't associate it with the key-punch operator."

"If the criminal who entrapped you had a room there, your whole explanation becomes rational. No wonder your shoes disappeared; not surprising that the door was locked on you. Maybe she was hiding in the broom cupboard opposite the door."

"But then why did the key turn up in my pocket?"

"You now say that you may have unconsciously removed the key when you stepped into the room, and put it into your pocket. But that isn't what happened at all. I think the criminal put it into your pocket when the jacket was hanging in your apartment in Yotsuya. The woman with the mole had access to that room; we know that, because she stole the diary. Reading it, she could predict your activities and play her tricks upon you."

"But how come the blood was my type?"

"She got the names of donors of your type from blood banks and must have collected from one of them—we know she made contact with at least four. Shinji, the man next to me, interviewed them all." Honda glanced at Shinji and then looked back at the old man.

"There's a lot I still don't fully understand. Why was there no sign of a struggle in any of the cases?"

"Perhaps the criminal used an anesthetic—chloroform or something like that. That would explain the sweet smell you noticed in both Fusako Aikawa's room and also Mitsuko Kosugi's."

"Chloroform. That fits."

"And the semen. That was collected from the blood donors, too."

"It's mad!" exclaimed Honda, tugging at his hair nervously. "Why me?" Watching him vacantly, Shinji realized that he had no more than a walk-on part in this drama.

The old man took out the notebook. "Your memory was very good. However, the criminal tore out the pages referring to Keiko Obana. That I can understand. What I cannot understand is why he tore out this page—the first one. Who was the woman described here?" The old man displayed the book to Honda. Looking at it, the prisoner's eyes gradually became hollow. It was as if his whole core had suddenly melted, leaving him no more than a soft doll. Watching the scene, Shinji felt even more of an outsider. Ichiro Honda knew whose name had appeared in that missing page . . . and so did the old man. The closeness of the room began to irritate him.

Honda opened his mouth for a few seconds, like a landed fish that finds the density of the air too much. "I can't remember who it was," he said at last. "Please give me time to think about it." From the way he would not meet their eyes,

Shinji realized that Honda knew the name of the woman very well but was not saying. The old man knew, too, he was certain. But the old man was silent. Without a word, he stood up, and gazed at the prisoner with sympathy before leaving the room.

On the way back to the office, Shinji wondered what the old man was going to do with the diary. What was the old man thinking about, his head on his chest, a cigar in his mouth?

Shinji, for his part, felt the slow stain of jealousy creep toward his heart. All of that diary that he wished to read was the passage referring to Michiko Ono.

3

About a week passed, and then there was a sudden development that took Shinji by surprise. Honda asked for an interview with the director of the prison and confessed his guilt, asking to be allowed to withdraw his appeal.

"Just what I feared," said the old man mysteriously. "We're off on our travels—get ready at once."

"Where are we going?"

"To Osaka. I've got to talk to the father-in-law of our client."

They left Tokyo that evening, and on the next day Shinji waited at the hotel whilst the old man went off to see Ichiro Honda's father-in-law. Before leaving, Hatanaka had been once more to Sugamo Prison, but Honda would say nothing about the missing page, merely asserting his guilt. Even Shinji understood that the reason for Honda's new stance was based upon the missing page at the front of the diary.

The old man had been to Osaka already, on his own, for five days from the day after the two of them had interviewed Honda in prison. He was uncommunicative about his trip, and Shinji did not feel that he could question him about it, confining himself to grumbling to Mutsuko Fujitsubo about the old man hogging the case now that it was getting interesting. He did at least gather that the objective had been to visit Honda's wealthy father-in-law as well as his wife. He had to admire the vigor of the old man, now over seventy, in undertaking this trip.

Now Shinji waited in the Osaka hotel. An hour passed, and the old man returned. Where had he been? Shinji did not ask, but got into the car and accompanied his chief to Ichiro Honda's wife's home.

They were met by the old housekeeper. She was plainly expecting them and conducted them immediately to the atelier at the back of the garden. Within, it was almost dark despite the brightness of the day outside; the only sound to be heard in the otherwise cavernous silence was the hum of the air conditioner. The old retainer took a long pole and slid back the cover to the skylight; immediately the room was flooded with light.

In the corner stood an old-fashioned iron bedstead, upon which a woman was lying. The housekeeper fetched a couple of wooden stools, which looked as if they were meant for children rather than adults, put them by the bed and invited the two men to sit on them with a silent gesture.

Shinji looked at Taneko, the wife of Ichiro Honda, for the first time. Although she was said to be under thirty, she looked like a sick woman in her forties. Was it his imagination that told him that the room was suffused with the smell of death, just like a cancer ward?

"Your husband has withdrawn his appeal," said the old man in measured tones. The woman on the bed made no reply. She seemed to be quite insensible to their presence. The old woman bent over the bed and whispered something in the woman's ear; there was no response, and she straightened up and shook her head at the two men.

The three of them gazed down at the sick woman; an invisible barrier seemed to separate her world from theirs. She lay without any sign of vitality, staring blankly at the ceiling, her blanket drawn up over her mouth. Only the whir of the air conditioner could be heard, marking the presence of reality and the passing of time. The minutes crept slowly by.

Eventually, Taneko moved a lifeless hand up toward her face, and the blanket slipped down to her throat. She stared at Shinji and the old man and laughed, but her face remained expressionless, giving her smile an eerie quality. And then Shinji saw it.

On the right base of her nose was a large mole, about the size of an Azuki bean! The mole of which he had heard so much!

It sat upon her face like the symbol of some revealed sin; gazing at the black stain, he muttered to himself, "Why did no one tell me that Honda's wife has a mole?"

Taneko stretched her hand toward the side table and slowly picked up a silver hand mirror. She gazed vacantly at her face in the mirror, and then slowly scooped up a handful of cold cream from the jar by the pillow and rubbed it over her cheek by the base of her nose. The mole began to blur and then finally vanished. What sort of a trick was this?

She then applied cream to her eyelids and dissolved the starchlike cosmetic that had given them a double-lidded form, reverting to narrow slits. The transformation complete, she replaced the mirror and lay back, her face once again a mask, hollow and unsmiling.

"So now you understand," said the old woman to Hatanaka and Shinji. She picked up the pole and made the room dark again. Silently the two men followed her out into the garden. Shinji looked back for one last time, but Taneko had once again pulled the blanket up over her face and lay as still as a corpse.

Back in the entrance hall to the main house, the old woman handed a notebook to the old man.

"This is her memo book in which she used to write before she got into her present state," she said. "You can see that it would be quite hopeless to conduct a handwriting test at present, so please use this as a sample of her handwriting. I feel sure that you will find that the writing matches that on the note by the Turkish bath girl. But you must promise me not to make this notebook public—not to anyone, not ever.

If you won't promise me that, I am going to throw it on the fire."

"Was it you," asked the old man, "who tore out the pages from the Huntsman's Log—the first page and the entry on the key-punch operator?"

"Yes, it was me."

"And was it you who put it in the apartment on the second floor of the house where Mitsuko Kosugi was killed?"

The old woman nodded. "The young mistress has gone beyond the reach of the law, and by doing what I have done my duty is now complete. I thought I ought to save Mr. Honda's life, so I went up to Tokyo six weeks ago and left the diary where you found it."

The old man smiled faintly as they took their leave.

Walking down the gentle paved slope that led to the station, Shinji was still stunned by the way things had turned out and said so. "I could have sworn it was the sister; how did you know?"

But the old man said nothing.

Suddenly, Shinji saw the pathos of the world. Going down the slope . . . on either side, modern houses with red-tiled roofs. Who knew what frugal lives were lived therein, what trifling quarrels took place? Banal and monotonous lives of everyday folk—what a contrast from the room from which he had just stepped! How real were they, the sick woman smelling of death and the man whose spirit had been broken in the condemned cell? Was it not all but a bad dream, occupying but one moment in this summer's heat?

He thought back to Yasue in the Turkish bath, to Tanikawa with his forced jollity in the chicken restaurant, to the medical student who always turned his back on him. How were these puppets in the curtained drama connected with that mad woman lying in bed, the blanket drawn over her face?

The old man hailed a taxi, and they got in.

But still . . ., thought Shinji.

Were not our experiences the same as those of Tiltil and Mytil, who found the bluebird at last in their own home? The woman with the mole, whom he had pursued so assiduously, had been in a cage all along.

Breaking into his reverie, Hatanaka spoke. "We're not out of the woods yet. I can't break my promise and use this notebook. We must find some other way to get the defendant out of jail."

Saying which, he vigorously shook the notebook that had been written by Taneko Honda.

Epilogue

(*A record written by the wife.*)

As I take up my pen, I feel rather strange. I remember the young journalist from the woman's magazine who used to come every day after my husband's arrest to ask me to write an article or give her an interview. My old maid never let her past the gate, but still she came every day for nearly three months.

But one day she stopped coming.

Oh well, an enthusiast like her probably got married or something!

Since she stopped calling at our gate every day, I won't say that I didn't become lonely, but nonetheless I must admit to being somewhat relieved. You see, I still had some unfinished business in Tokyo, and I wanted to be able to get away. . . .

When the news of my husband's arrest reached me, I was painting in my atelier.

The basic color of the painting was red.

What would my Chicago analyst, Dr. John Wells, have said if he could have seen it?

He'd have put it down to my repressed sexual urges again, I imagine.

It was the local policeman who came to inform me. He had a search warrant to go through my husband's belongings. But he was quite perfunctory about it.

Maybe it was out of respect for my father. Or else they already had more than enough evidence to secure a conviction. Anyway, they didn't disturb us too much.

It was the local police chief who looked into my atelier. He was very reserved about it and didn't even notice the half-full bottle of chloroform that was in amongst my paints and turpentine. I wasn't even trying to hide it—why bother? Their attitude toward me was one of sympathy mixed with curiosity. . . .

They took it for granted that I was distraught at the discovery that my husband was a murderer with perverse tastes. That suited me very well; I hardly had to act at all; all I had to do was lie on my bed pretending to be a woman struck speechless by shock.

After all, that's the way the relatives of criminals are, isn't it? The worse the crime, the more they try to bury themselves away from ordinary human society. That suited me very well.

My worst fear was the press. What if they took my photograph? But, perhaps out of sympathy for me as the innocent victim of my husband's crimes, they were tasteful enough to leave me alone. Some of the gutter-press tried to get my photo, but I foiled them by staying indoors. So the only photos that were published were of me when I was twenty and striking dramatic poses during my short career as an actress, or else of me as a high school girl wearing a sailor suit, my hair in pigtails. So that was all right—no way in which I could be recognized.

My next worry was that I might be summoned to the court to appear as a witness. I decided to lose enough weight to change my appearance during the few months leading up to the trial. I started to starve myself; after a few weeks, I caught sight of my legs and was stunned. What lovely legs I used to have! All tanned and well shaped, with firm muscles, just like the legs of an antelope. How proud I had been of them! I always used to wear the shortest possible skirts when playing tennis, just to show them off. I used to let my skirts ride up, letting men see how brown my thighs were, right up to the briefest of pants, which I always wore. And underneath, right down to where the pants ended—Oh, if they could have seen how white were the secret places of my body!

But now they were like the colorless bones of a skeleton. I pulled my negligee up; the color was the same on both my legs and my private parts. They looked like the legs of a Jew in a concentration camp.

I took off the negligee and looked at myself naked; I really was becoming like a skeleton with only a few wisps of hair in the middle!

But it was affecting my health; I was taking purgatives to get my weight down and soon became too feeble even to open my mouth to issue instructions to the housekeeper. I even lacked the strength to pick up the blanket when it slipped off the bed. I was smoking heavily to repress my appetite; my right hand became a nicotine-stained claw. Having no strength, I would frequently drop my cigarette and set my bedding asmolder. The housekeeper scolded me on such occasions, but what could I do?

If I did start a fire, the atelier would be razed to its foundations, and then that would lead to my ruin. . . . But I had to keep on smoking.

I dreaded that the housekeeper would stop getting me my cigarettes. I needed the smoke of those hot, dry leaves with their pungent smell and billowing, purple-colored smoke; I needed them to help the loneliness, terror, and obsessions of my lonely bed.

For a time I fasted on no more than a little thin gruel, but I needed more substance to make the cigarettes taste good, so I would occasionally take a little breast of chicken fried in a good-quality oil or else eat a quarter of a sugar-sprinkled doughnut.

Eventually, I couldn't hold on to anything. I dropped everything I touched—a water jug, an ashtray full of butts, even the expensive antique German fountain pen that I had bought in Chicago.

But I couldn't give up the cigarettes.

I always kept a big tin of Westminster by my bed, but it soon got empty. The old housekeeper used to complain about the smoke-filled atmosphere and open the windows. One cold February night, she didn't close them properly, and the draft was freezing me, so I got up and tried to shut them. But I just didn't have the strength.

That was when I was weakest, I think.

In those days, I was not bothered by visits from the dead. No, it was sex that dominated my mind: his sex, and my sex.

What dreams do men have who have been soldiers and who have killed? What do they think, falling asleep alone at night, of those whom they overcame after struggling hand to hand? Or those ancient warriors, naked between the sheets, dreaming of their youth and well-oiled nakedness, the bulging muscles of youth, the struggles ... now all gone. What did they think of in bed?

I thought of the touch of his naked body, drenched with the sweat of the women that he had mounted. . . .

I thought of myself, naked and giving myself to men to collect the evidence I needed. My palms still seemed to feel the flesh of those men to whom I had submitted. . . .

Well, at any rate, it turned out that I would not have to appear in court. A clerk of the court came to see me, armed with a tape recorder to ask me about our married life together. He mainly asked about our sexual relations, or rather lack of them, since my husband became impotent with me. It seemed that our family doctor had already been questioned, so all of the questions were very much to the point. There were a few medical terms that I didn't understand, but all I had to do was nod.

When he came to the word *spasm* he used the German word *kampf*, blushing as he spoke.

Perhaps he had a lascivious imagination; perhaps he imagined me naked and lying under him.

I can't blame him or our family doctor, because how could they know the real reason for my fear of pregnancy?

Nobody knows . . . except us, and the alcoholic doctor in Mexico who swindled us out of two thousand dollars. . . . Only we three know about the baby born without bones, the baby we disposed of.

Mad, that's what it was, to go sightseeing in Mexico in the ninth month of my pregnancy. Why didn't we go back to Japan instead? Then we would never have fallen into the clutches of that doctor. . . . Then I would not have had to dye my hands with the blood of my infant.

And two weeks after the birth. I had recovered enough for sex. I lay under my husband, in his arms, in a hotel built like a mountain hut by the side of a lake.

We were just reaching our climax . . . and I went into a spasm. My body gripped his like a vise . . . he screamed with pain . . . I was in agony, too. Somehow, I managed to get hold of the phone, locked together as we were.

That boorish fathead of a doctor, looking at the nude yellow couple clasped in the first embrace shown in marital textbooks . . . just as if we were a pair of copulating monkeys or dogs. Because of the pain, we didn't feel embarrassed. He injected a depressant, and eventually we were able to separate.

Well, when we got back to Chicago, Dr. John Wells diagnosed the reason for my convulsive spasm. It was, he said, a fear syndrome directed against pregnancy. He said the same thing would happen in the future if I made love to my husband, and that it would happen just as he was about to ejaculate. He said, "It's like having a nervous pain in your muscle. You'll get it even if you use contraceptives. You'll get it with other men, too." Unless I could overcome my fear of pregnancy. As it was all in English, it was less embarrassing to listen to.

Thus began the agony of the centaur. Does not the head wish to make love to a woman, whilst the lower parts can only cover a mare?

Or we were like the starving figure in Greek mythology, buried up to his neck with plates of delicious food just in front of his nose.

First we would look at each other's bodies . . . exchange caresses . . . at last give up in desperation. Always so fruitlessly tired . . . always, the stain of our sweat on the sheets, full of the sorrowful smell that symbolized our barren love.

The doctor thought that my fear of childbirth was due to the failure of my first pregnancy—we had put it about that I had had a miscarriage in Mexico—and suggested that all would be well if we changed our environment. But my husband and I, knowing the real cause, knew better. Our future as man and wife had ended in a brick wall.

My husband found a post in Tokyo, and we came back to Japan. We lived apart, except for Saturday nights.

And so, once a week, we would sometimes search for each other's body in the darkness, dreaming that a miracle might occur. However, after a while, we gave up. My husband told me that when he was with me, he was no longer a complete man.

With a weak smile like an old man's, he would stroke the thick hair on his chest and say ruefully, "I am impotent. I have lost all interest in women. Sometimes I go to a strip show or look at nudes in magazines, though. That's about it, I'm afraid."

And like a fool, I pitied him, still young and handsome, and yet already impotent.

When we first met, he was a melancholic man, but in spite of that he was very quick-witted and seemed to be able easily to make others believe in love between men and women. I remember him well, standing in front of the red-brick university building in Chicago, wearing a red woolen shirt; he struck such a fine pose, his head slightly to one side, that he seemed to match the American scenery around him, and I immediately fell in love with him. I always loved him—the first man I ever knew.

So, one day, when our separation had gone on for six months (and it was my idea originally; I thought that if we were together every night, the torture would be too much), I was overcome by a sudden desire to see him. I got into my Mercedes and set off for Tokyo without ado. All those six hundred kilometers on the road I was in a dream.

It was almost dawn when I got to the Toyo Hotel, where he was staying. It was still winter, and outside it was cold and dark. I parked in front of the hotel and switched off the headlamps. I sat and finished my cigarette, looking at the hotel; later, when it was not too early, I would go in. And then suddenly I saw a familiar figure getting out of a taxi; surely it couldn't be ... but yes, it was my husband.

He paid his fare; his face was expressionless under the lamplight. And somehow, looking at him, I saw about him a dark shadow, suggestive of tiredness after secret lovemaking. Why didn't I follow him immediately and accost him? I still don't know.

If only he had come back ten minutes earlier! Or later, when I was more composed and could have approached him; we would have had our customarily meaningless chat; a cup of tea together, and I would have said good-bye.

After all, there's no contending with fate, I know that. It was fate, wasn't it, which brought me there at that precise time, to turn out the headlights and find myself in a position just overlooking the entrance to the hotel at the moment that he came back.

I stayed in the car, my coat collar turned up, rubbing my feet together to keep them warm. At that sort of hour, if one has something on one's mind, you go into a sort of trance without sleeping. I wonder why.

The sun came up, and the first car in the lot had its engine started, clouds of white exhaust filling the icy air. Finally, I could bring myself to move, and I drove back to Osaka without taking any sleep on the way.

That weekend, my husband came back as usual. I greeted him as if nothing had happened, and we spent our usual weekend together. I made no attempt to cross-examine him or catch him out.

For the next two weeks, I resolutely closed my mind to what I had seen and immersed myself in my painting. Even if my husband did have a mistress, I thought, it was my duty to forgive him. But nonetheless I could not resist the temptation, and two weeks later I drove up to Tokyo again.

This time, I arrived in Yokohama about noon and parked my car at a hotel near the seafront, one which usually has a lot of foreign guests. Then I rented an inconspicuous car; I had decided, against the voice of reason, to spy on my husband.

Words are not enough for me to explain the bottomless sense of humiliation and despair that crept over me when I saw the Huntsman's Log at my husband's hideout at Yotsuya.

I wish I had never found the key to that apartment in his jacket pocket. I wish I had not had my maid get a spare key made. I wish I had not followed him there. . . .

It would have been much better for me to have known nothing.

It wasn't all his different women who made me feel that I could not forgive my husband. About those victims I did not particularly care. I could not forgive him because he had listed me as his first victim. And I could not forgive him because he was not afraid to make any of those other women pregnant.

This was how he described what to me was a most precious night, the first night we made love, in the summer holidays:

"It was cramped in the car, but I enjoyed the unnatural posture this forced upon our lovemaking. Her pants off, her skirt pulled up, one leg over the back of the front seat. It made her body tight to enter, which was extra pleasure. Good breasts; she pulled her sweater up, and I did not bother to remove her bra, but pulled it down (though later she took it off herself) and I could see them in the moonlight as I worked on her. Later, she turned over, and asked me to enter her from the back, which I did. Used her mouth on me, too.

"I had invested all my earnings from my part-time job in that old Chevrolet, and this experience made the investment fully worthwhile.

"Keen on foreplay, and definitely not a virgin."

Was that how he saw our tender and romantic congress? And what did he mean by saying "not a virgin"? I had never known any man before.

A few months later, I read of the suicide of the key-punch operator who was one of the victims described in his diary.

I went to her sister, Tsuneko Obana, at her apartment in Omori. The reason was that I wanted to make sure that my suspicions about the cause of the suicide were correct.

I think it was seeing the mole on her nose that made me decide to plot against my husband. That kind of defect attracts one's attention, even though one feels sorry for the person who has it. As she spoke, her anger was obvious; those eyes of hers glared through her double eyelids.

"My sister was just a stupid girl. But the man who caused her doom . . . he wasn't stupid, and I can never forgive him, never, never."

How I envied her then; she had such a clear motive for revenge against my husband. I began to wish to change myself into her, to savor the sweetness of revenge.

I had had some cards printed that passed me off as a correspondent for a women's magazine. She was a simple and straitlaced woman, so it was easy for me to deceive her. I offered her money to write an article on her sister's death, and I also suggested that with my cooperation she could track down the man responsible.

"Do you really think we could?" She looked at me anxiously as she said this, but I was in no doubt as to her hatred for my husband. So she ended up accepting my offer. Of course, I told her to tell no one about me, because this would get me into trouble with my magazine, particularly if some other magazine got wind of our project and stole it.

Based on the diary of her sister, I suggested that she go to the bar Boi and trace the man who had sung with her. Everything went without a hitch; it all seemed too easy. She trusted me completely and did exactly what I said. Everything she found out she wrote down and gave to me.

But still I was not satisfied. Indeed, the more our plan succeeded, the more irritated I became. I was getting jealous of this woman; somehow, her activities seemed to create a re-lationship between her and my husband. Of course, really I was at this time beginning to think abnormally. Jealousy is a powerful thing. And my lust for sex is so strong.

So gradually, deep down inside myself, I began to wish that I could become Tsuneko Obana and partake of her longing for revenge against my husband.

And the semen. That was a good idea of mine, I think. You may say that it only amounted to circumstantial evi-dence, but think of it this way. If, by any chance, my hus-band was able to clear himself despite my efforts, at least the police would not turn their attention toward me or Tsuneko Obana, for how could women produce semen?

And when I started to collect semen from those men, it became central to the meaning of my life. Women, after all, are creatures who take semen from men . . . and my husband would give me none. So it was poetic justice, in a way. . . . I was punishing my husband for not giving me the semen that is a woman's right. . . .

But was I really punishing my husband; was that all? Maybe it was just an excuse to collect semen.

And the blood. Leaving blood of my husband's group under the nails of my victims—that was clever, wasn't it?

*   *   *

Well, my urges became stronger and stronger, and so did my jealousy of Tsuneko Obana. I led her on, used her as a puppet; she did everything I wanted, but even that did not give me full pleasure. I sent her to A.M.U. to check the blood type, which of course I knew perfectly well all along. I got her to phone the Toyo Hotel with an assumed voice. Poor cat's-paw; she thought she was discovering things, which were perfectly well known to me all along. And just in case anyone ever checked up, it would be the woman with the mole that they would hunt.

But her usefulness was past. Now I must take the law into my own hands, and she could prove an obstacle. She knew too much. So I suggested that she should move out of her apartment and take another in her sister's name. She had to vanish for good; I had to become Tsuneko Obana, and then I would acquire the fullest motive for revenge upon my husband.

Dr. John Wells would have attributed my lust for revenge against my husband to repressed sexual desire, I suppose. Those psychiatrists have one-track minds. . . .

I set my trap with the semen I took from those men and the Rh-negative blood I stole from the cosmetics salesman in the inn, whom I chloroformed first. I also used chloroform on my victims so that they did not resist when I strangled them.

* * *

The woman in Kinshicho. She was just a sort of hors d'oeuvre to begin the process of terror on my husband. So there was no need to leave blood under her fingernails.

In the case of Fusako Aikawa in Koenji, I chloroformed my husband as he lay sleeping at my side and took his blood. I was worried about that blood, because it coagulated in the test tube on the way to Tokyo, even though I had packed it in dry ice. Would it fool them? I could but try.

Well, I went to visit Fusako Aikawa, but before I could make my escape, my husband turned up! I hid in the closet until he left, but my heart was freezing with terror. However, it was all right in the end, but I had to make a quick getaway just in case he called the police.

As for Mitsuko Kosugi, she was in my pay all along. She didn't mind kissing my husband at Tokyo Tower, prudish little girl that she was, because she knew that I was watching. I had to confront my husband, invisibly, as it were, to terrify him the more. Did it work, I wonder? But I doubt if she ever had sex with him; she wasn't the type. She had to die anyhow, poor girl.

The trick with the blade in the wardrobe; now that was neat. It drew blood, just as I intended, though I thought there was no better than a one-in-ten chance. Frankly, when I saw how well it worked, I was a bit scared. Was there not some other invisible hand moving me in my pursuit of revenge?

All that I did thus became a sort of ceremony, one that I had to perform regardless of whether it worked or not. Killing three or four people thus became nothing to me; my psychology knew no limitation.

So much for Dr. John Wells and his comfortable theories. He can forget his statistics, forget about suppressed sexual drives. What do people like him know?

November 5.
At the Minami apartment in Kinshicho.

I waited for two hours in my car.

At three A.M. *I was ready. I put on a mask, the kind one wears when one has a cold, and got out of the car. Even though I had looked the place over by daytime, I still stumbled over the lumber stacked in the lane.*

She woke up when I went in, but was still half-asleep. Her eyes were swollen and there was saliva around her mouth.

"I want to talk about Sobra," I said. She just rolled over and turned her back to me.

I pressed the chloroform-soaked handkerchief to her nose; the liquid ran down my right hand.

A little struggle, and she was unconscious.

I stripped her naked and produced a syringe without a needle.

As I slipped it between her thighs and began to inject the semen, suddenly I began a convulsive spasm.

A chill of death settled over the room. I buried my fingernails in her body. The room smelt of chestnut flowers.

I passed the drawstring of her sleeping gown around her neck.

Somewhere, my husband, too, was bending over the body of a victim.

As I drew the drawstring tight, I got another convulsion.

The power of my hands . . . I pulled with all my might.

Her face turned purple. It was done. I lost consciousness for a while. . . .

My husband's hunting days were limited to Tuesdays and Thursdays, I found.

After the first time, it was easy. I, a passive woman who normally trembles with fear at the slightest thing, drew closer and closer to my victims.

Why am I writing this? I began to want to do it when I heard that my husband had been sentenced to death.

That woman student I hired—she did her job well. She set up her canvas at the museum to lure my husband as I suggested, and it worked. At Tokyo Tower, she was my decoy; she knew that I was watching from the shadows and was not afraid to kiss him. She summoned him to her room late at night; she was not afraid, for I told her that I would be there.

She had to die, poor, blameless thing. At the very least my

husband deserves to die for the murder of that innocent woman. For husband and wife are one, are they not? So it really doesn't matter if he, my better half, goes to the gallows in my place.

Today, my father phoned to say that the bed in the hospital is now ready for me. By tomorrow, I'll be in the hospital. Tomorrow and tomorrow and tomorrow . . . all those mornings, I will awake in a hospital bed. It's my destiny.

And some day, perhaps when I am long gone, this atelier will be torn down. They will rip up the concrete foundations, and what will they find? Human bones; no more, I daresay. And certainly the mole will have vanished in the decomposition. Nothing to identify Tsuneko Obana by. Unless science has made progress by then; perhaps they will detect the aftermath of a mole. Tsuneko Obana. I had to do it. I had to become her.

But all that is in the future.

Today, I know that I am going farther and farther away from myself, drawn by those invisible powers that have controlled me more and more of late. Those sounds in my head—how I wish they would go away! Perhaps they can do something about it in the hospital. If a policeman came to question me today, I know that I could give him no answer.

And talking of the future, what does it hold in store for me? Today I am all skin and bones, but in ten or twenty years' time it will be different. I shall be a fat nymphomaniac lying in a hospital bed, eating chocolates or my own excretur—what does it matter? In the corner of the psychiatric ward, I will be known as the woman who winds her drawstring around the bedstead and pulls with all her might.

Nearly 4 P.M. Time for me to become Tsuneko Obana again.

I get my makeup box. With skill I fix my eyes; there, nobody will recognize my face now! Carefully I brush black ink onto the base of my nose.

Inside my head, as persistent as a sutra, I hear Tsuneko Obana's monologue:

"Silly, silly little girl. Don't say you cried in his arms; don't tell me that you were crushed under his body...."

Shinji closed the notebook and gazed at the old man, who was impassively smoking his cigar.

"It will take time, of course," Hatanaka said, "but that should be enough."

"But can you use it? Your promise ..."

"From which I regard myself as being released. That old housekeeper hanged herself after we left. I half expected it; do you remember what she said? 'My duty is now complete.' Well, that feudal type, you know it can only mean one thing. A pity not more Japanese are like her nowadays."

"And you did not try to stop her?"

"Ah well, you are so young, you see. You modern people; I wonder if in time you will become real Japanese again! No. To frustrate the loyalty of a retainer is a sin for which one should burn in hell! She wrote a note to me, however: 'Everything is now in your hands.'

"And the wife is now in a mental home, of course. *Non compos mentis*—and this notebook proves it. They can never bring her to trial—if they try, I will take great pleasure in defending her. They doubt if she will ever recover her physical strength, too."

The old man blew a smoke ring, and suddenly Shinji was reconciled to the grinding routines of the law. To work for such a man, and someday, perhaps, to become like him . . .

It was at the end of October that Ichiro Honda was finally released from prison. He gazed appreciatively at the autumn tints and breathed deeply of the chill wind that blew against the gray stones of the court building that he had put behind him.